Willie Hogg

Willie Hogg

Robin Jenkins

Polygon
EDINBURGH

© Robin Jenkins 1993

Published by Polygon
22 George Square
EDINBURGH

Set in Garamond by ROM-Data Corporation Ltd, Falmouth, Cornwall, England
Printed and bound in Great Britain by Hartnolls Ltd, Bodmin, Cornwall

British Library Cataloguing In Publication Data
Jenkins, Robin
    Willie Hogg
    I. Title
    823.914 F

ISBN 0 7486 6152 2

The Publisher acknowledges subsidy from the Scottish Arts Council towards
the publication of this volume.

To Charlie and Selina,
lovers of Glasgow,
and also, as always,
in memory of May

Part One

The nurses used to joke that even patients who had died in agony had happy smiles on their faces because it was wee Willie Hogg wheeling them to the mortuary. If anyone could get them into heaven, it was Willie; and certainly if it had been left to him he would have admitted them all, though he himself did not believe in it, having been taught in the Socialist Sunday school that such a place could not possibly exist. Even as a boy pledged to reject promises of eternal bliss he had been remarkable for his good nature and obliging ways, if not for his quickness of mind. His more percipient teachers, though, had soon come to realise that he usually arrived at a sound conclusion, whether it was a sum in vulgar fractions or a matter of morality: it just took him a bit longer.

When he grew up and became a soldier in North Africa he had never risen above the rank of private. His cheerful acceptance of menial tasks like cleaning out latrines had earned him praise and affection, but not promotion. He was marked down as willing but unambitious. After the War he had no difficulty in regaining his old job as porter in the Glasgow Royal Infirmary where everybody, from patients to consultants, soon discovered that his usefulness did not end with his ordinary tasks like helping to lift heavy patients or wheeling corpses to the mortuary. His very presence at a scene of crisis had a calming effect. His was one of those fortunate natures that steady the world. He never grumbled or looked for someone to blame. Duties outside the scope of his contract were undertaken with a meekness that mesmerised the most militant of trade unionists: whatever Willie was he was no scab or boss's toady. Indeed, he was a zealous union man himself, paying his dues on time and attending all meetings, though he spoke at none. When he retired, at sixty-five, everybody subscribed to his farewell present: a television set. He had asked for this in place of a gold watch. The set he already had was defective. This hadn't bothered him much but it did his wife Maggie who often watched till all the channels had gone off the air and even after that.

He had married Maggie when he was twenty-three and she twenty-one. Faithful to his Socialist Sunday school principles he could not have a minister of the gospel at his wedding. Besides, in spite of his pug nose, he was a romantic at heart and wanted to be married according to the old Scottish custom of declaration. Maggie had raised no objections, though for years afterwards she was still puzzled that there had been no one in a dog collar present or anyone holding a Bible. For it has to be said that if Willie at school had been thought a slow learner Maggie's teachers had despaired of ever teaching her anything at all. At first they had been impressed by her continual expression of rapt attention until they discovered that she was really in a day-dream or dwam. In those days inattentive or unresponsive pupils had been leathered in the foolish hope that it would make them keen and bright, but little Margaret McCrae had been spared. No child in the school had been less troublesome or more pathetic. It was agreed that the poor girl wasn't all there, but where she was remained a mystery.

So why had Willie married her? Her sister Elspeth, five years younger and therefore only sixteen at the time, a fierce-eyed evangelistical girl, had taken him aside and, in her forceful way, reminded him that since he himself was not the brainiest man in the Cowcaddens and Margaret was little better than a moron, what children they might have were bound to be weak-minded, to the point of idiocy. Why then was he marrying her sister? It wasn't that Margaret had beauty to make up for her lack of intelligence. He could see for himself that she was flat-chested and thin-legged. If she did have a certain sweetness in her face it was because there was nothing in her mind. (Elspeth herself was tall and buxom, with legs like a football player's and a face no one would ever call sweet.) If he was under the delusion that the McCraes had money that he hoped to get his hands on then he was very much mistaken. If he took Margaret that was all he was taking, and God help him.

Willie had been characteristically humble but resolute in his reply. He did not say that he loved Maggie, for he was not absolutely sure that he did, but he was fond enough of her to want to look after her. If she was as useless as Elspeth had portrayed her then she very much needed looking after. Not that he had agreed she was useless. There could be riches in her that kindness and patience would uncover.

Elspeth was afterwards to accuse him of getting married without a religious ceremony, out of spite. She never forgave him, and when she emigrated to America soon after the War wrote letters only to Maggie, never to him. They were written as if to a ten year-old, a backward one at that. Maggie, who could be stubborn, insisted on writing the replies herself, with no assistance from him. They were like what a backward ten year-old might have written. It wasn't long therefore before this peculiar correspondence dwindled and then died.

The time came when Willie and Maggie were left on their own, except for distant relatives whom they seldom saw. Both Willie's parents had died before his marriage and soon after that Maggie's father was found dead in bed from a heart attack. She didn't seem to miss him much but when her mother followed him in less than a year, killed by pneumonia, she was disconsolate for a long time and, in a way that he sympathised with, blamed Willie. When a person you loved dearly died unexpectedly you had to blame someone, so he tholed her tearful accusations and grew still fonder of her.

As it happened they never had any children. Whose fault it was they never tried to find out. It was a disappointment to Willie but he was never sure what it meant to Maggie. She liked being allowed to take out a neighbour's baby in its pram or hold it in her arms, but she never expressed regret at not having one of her own.

They lived for many years up a close in the Cowcaddens, in a room-and-kitchen with no bathroom and a shared toilet on the landing. Eventually they had been rehoused, in a council flat in the same district. This time they had a proper bathroom. Willie's pay was never as high as the national average, though he worked as many hours of overtime as he could get. They managed well enough as long as he took charge of their finances. One day he came home and found that she had ordered a new lounge suite, a magnificence of red and black leather, costing over £2000. Luckily it hadn't yet been delivered. It had let him know that though she lived simply and frugally she had visions of splendour and luxury. It broke his heart that he could not afford to let her have it. In any case, as she herself penitently pointed out, it would have been too massive for their small living-room. To compensate her he bought her a statuette, of a shepherdess with a lamb at her feet, in pink and white porcelain.

Every Sunday afternoon whatever the weather he accompanied her to her mother's grave in Janefield Cemetery. It was her father's too but she never mentioned him, though David McCrae had seemed to Willie a decent if dim little man. She begged Willie to pay for a headstone, with a wee winged angel on it, and though it was against his principles (for if he didn't believe in heaven how could he believe in angels?) he was willing to oblige her, provided her father's name was inscribed on it too. She sulked but acquiesced: though as she knelt arranging the flowers she had brought it was only to her mother she spoke. It brought tears to Willie's eyes as he watched her kneeling there, her grey head cocked to the side like a bird listening for worms. She told her mother a lot about Elspeth in America but had to make it up for it had been many years since her sister had last written. She said that Elspeth, who had been a clerkess in the local carpet factory before emigrating, was now manageress of a large store in New York, with a staff of hundreds. Once she asked him to confirm it. Feeling more of a fool than a liar he too had talked to Mrs McCrae. Maggie had been pleased with him.

2

It would have been unfair and untrue to say that he had to have a refuge from Maggie. If you had suggested it he would have been offended. But just the same there was such a place where he gladly went, in his old age, though always to be sure with Maggie's blessing. This was the pub, *The Airlie Arms*, in Wallace Street, where all the buildings were under sentence of demolition. It was famous for its ornate Victorian fittings and for having been owned at one time by a famous Scottish footballer. Here for some years after his retirement Willie and a small band of cronies, pensioners like himself, met every Tuesday and Thursday from three o'clock to five. In a cosy secluded corner they played dominoes, and discussed the affairs of the world. They made their pints last out the two hours, for a pint was all they could afford, except on special occasions. The present owner, Jack Adams, didn't mind the old 'philosophers' as he called them, so long as they stayed away on Friday and Saturday nights when the pub was thronged with real drinkers.

Counting Willie himself there were five of them, or perhaps it would have been truer to say four, for the fifth, Duncan Forsyth, was not a regular and did not live in the district. Where he did live the others did not know. Sometimes they wondered if he had a settled abode at all, for he looked as if he slept in backyard middens, judging by the dirt on his long raincoat and the smell off it. He wore a soiled cloth cap pulled low over his ears. The bristle on his chin was white and he gave his age as seventy-two. According to his vague accounts he spent his days wandering about the streets of the city, visiting places like the People's Palace and the Art Galleries where he got in free but wasn't made welcome, and cemeteries which were also free and where no one minded.

He came creeping into the Arms one bitterly cold January afternoon and was at once ordered out by Pete Shivas, the barman on duty: tramps weren't allowed. Willie had protested, though he had never seen the man before. He had got up and welcomed him, heedless of Pete's grumbles, and bought him a pint.

His friends at the time hadn't approved of his philanthropy, because of the stink off the newcomer, but they had soon relented. Duncan had said very little and sipped the beer as if it were Drambuie. He did give his name, and while the others were discussing the crisis of Communism in Poland, interposed the shy remark that his wife Martha had died three years ago. That stopped instantly their talk about Lech Walesa. Here was a Scotsman, as old as themselves, more deserving of their attention and sympathy. They asked tactful questions but got meagre, diffident answers. They got the impression that he had had a sorrowful past. As for his future they could see for themselves that he had none at all.

After that first visit it was five weeks before he appeared again, still wearing the same coat and cap. He did not say where he had been or what he had been doing. This time he paid for his own beer but it was only half a pint.

The three other regulars besides Willie himself were Charlie McCann, seventy-six, Alec Struan, seventy-two, and Angus McPhie, seventy.

Charlie was the proudest and most touchy man Willie had ever met, though he had been a poorly paid street sweeper all his working life. He had once almost lost his job for banging with his brush the roof of a car whose driver had thrown rubbish out of the window on to the street that Charlie had just swept. It was reported in the *Daily Chronicle*, with a picture of Charlie and his brush. He would have sued the newspaper if he had had the money. His wife had died in childbirth three years after they were married: the child had died too. He had never married again and lived by himself in a room-and-kitchen with Polly his cat. He suffered from a bad back and had had to give up wearing socks because he couldn't bend low enough to put them on. He was almost bald and had big brown age marks on his scalp where Gorbachev the Russian leader had birth marks. His friends suspected he was proud of this similarity but did not dare chaff him about it.

Angus McPhie was small and fat. He had been born on the island of Barra and brought to Glasgow by his parents when he was a baby. He tried to speak with a Hebridean lilt and liked to stick in a Gaelic word or two. He had been brought up a Catholic and still considered himself one though he seldom attended chapel. This was because Nellie his Protestant wife protested when he did, but also because, so he said earnestly, he was allergic to the smell of candles. He did not like jokes about the Pope except those he told himself. He had worked for the gas company.

Alec Struan was a retired postman, with fallen arches. He had a great interest in the oddities of history. 'Did you ken, Angus, that when the Pope in Rome heard that King Billy had won the Battle of the Byne – he did not know it but he gave it its contemporary pronunciation – 'he had a' the candles lit and a' the bells rung in the Vatican in celebration?' 'Aye, Alec, I ken, for this is the sixth time you've told me.' Though she was over seventy herself Alec's wife Sadie had her hair dyed carroty red and went dancing with a variety of male partners. He claimed that she had his permission but his friends doubted it. Sadie wasn't a woman who needed permission. He had a number of grandchildren whose photographs he showed to people whether they were interested or not. He maintained he was happy with his lot, but how could he be, with painful feet, a wife like Sadie, and a conviction that the world would be destroyed by nuclear war in the next ten years?

Maggie always saw to it that Willie was presentable before he set out. 'What kind of wife will they think you've got, Willie Hogg, if they see you wi' shoes needing polished?' And, ignoring his protests, she would go down on her knees and polish his shoes until a cat could have seen its face in them. Once, when she wasn't well, he said he'd stay at home with her. To his dismay she had seized her hair like a madwoman and screamed that if he refused to go because of her she'd go out and throw herself under a bus. She knew, she screamed, that she had been a drag on him all their married life and before that too, and now when she was trying to make it up to him he wouldn't let her. He had done his best to pacify her but the beer that afternoon had tasted sour and he was told off for mistaking a double-five for a double-six.

3

Willie and Maggie rarely received personal letters, so one Tuesday, early in November, when one came addressed to Mrs William Hogg they were both intrigued, especially as it had an American stamp.

'It must be from Elspeth,' said Maggie, 'but it's no' her hand-writing.'

The writing on the envelope was small and careful, whereas Elspeth's had always been big and bold.

'You read it, Willie,' said Maggie.

He knew why she hesitated to open the envelope and read the letter. She did not want to find out that she had been telling her mother fibs about Elspeth.

'It's addressed to you, Maggie.'

'But I'd like you to read it, Willie.'

'If that's what you want, hen.'

There was only one sheet of notepaper. The address at the top astonished him:

Red Bluffs Apostolic Mission
Broken Arrow Navajo Reservation
Holbrook
Arizona.

The signature at the bottom was Randolph Hansen.

Surely it could have nothing to do with Elspeth. Who was Randolph Hansen?

'What does it say, Willie?'

'It's from somebody ca'd Randolph Hansen.'

'Randolph? I don't ken onybody ca'd that. Except that big man that acts in cowboy pictures. And his name's no' Hansen.'

And it was hardly likely that Randolph Scott had written to her.

Willie read it, at first to himself, in case it contained news that would distress Maggie and would have to be modified before it was given to her.

Dear Mrs Hogg

I am writing to you without the knowledge of my wife Elspeth, your sister. She is in charge of the above-mentioned mission. I am sorry to have to tell you that she is dying of cancer. She believes it is a matter between herself and God and is no one else's goddamn business. I found your name and address among her papers. I do not suppose you would wish to undertake so long and expensive a journey, but you may wish to write.

Yours very sincerely

Randolph Hansen.

'What does it say, Willie?'

He read it again, aloud this time, leaving out nothing.

It was too much for her to take in. 'Read it again, Willie, mair slowly.'

He did so, still unable to keep incredulity out of his voice.

Maggie was shaking her head. 'Are you sure it's for me?'

'I think so. It's addressed to Mrs Hogg, and there can't be all that many Elspeths in America.'

'But oor Elspeth was always strong and healthy.'

So she had been but cancer struck at random. Elspeth would be about sixty-two now.

'And what would she be doing in charge of a mission?'

Ramming her idea of God down the throats of unfortunate heathens. But he agreed with Maggie that it was preposterous.

'Mind you, she was always religious. She won prizes in the Bible class and she was a Sunday school teacher for years.'

Yes, when he came to think of it, Elspeth had had it in her to become a missionary.

'Navajo? What kind of word's that?'

'The Navajos are an Indian tribe.'

'Indians? Like that Gandhi that never wore troosers?'

'No. Red Indians. The kind you see in Wild West films.'

'With feathers in their hair?'

'Aye, that lot.'

'But they're savages. They bury people up to the neck in sand.'

'I don't think they do that nooadays, if they ever did.'

'I don't understand a' this, Willie. Will you explain it to me?'

'I'll try, hen. God knows how it's come aboot but it seems Elspeth runs a Christian mission among Navajo Indians in a place ca'd Holbrook in Arizona in America. She seems to have a husband ca'd Randolph Hansen and—' his voice faltered—'she's dying of cancer.'

'I don't believe a word of it. I'm five years aulder than her and I've no' got cancer.'

'No, but you've got a weak heart and puff and pant when you come up stairs too fast. A body can have cancer at ony age. Babies are born wi' it.'

'What does he mean, this Randolph Hansen, saying it's naebody else's goddamn business? What's goddamn?'

'It's an American swear word.'

'Why's he swearing in a letter that says his wife's got cancer?'

'He'd be upset, Maggie.'

'Why is *she* in charge of this mission? Why is it no' him?'

Willie had been wondering about that too.

'I don't believe she's married. She would have written and telt me.'

No, Maggie, she would not. She gave up writing to you long ago.

'Whit are we going to do, Willie?'

What indeed? They had a little money saved up but not nearly enough to pay their fares. Besides, Maggie's heart would never be able to stand up to such a long and exhausting journey: not to mention her mind.

She had gone quiet. She took the letter and put it in the pocket of her apron. 'Where are my specs?' she asked.

He found them for her.

'I'd like to be by mysel' for a while, Willie, if you don't mind.'

'I don't mind, hen.'

She often retreated into the bedroom to be alone.

'Wait till I put on the electric fire.'

'I can do that for mysel', thank you.'

'Will you be a' right?'

'Why shouldn't I be a' right? I'm not a wean, though you often treat me like one.'

When she had gone into the bedroom he looked for the school atlas he had bought in Woolworth's. He found it and turned to America. Arizona was easy to find but not Holbrook. The name was printed so small it must be a place of little importance. It looked as if it was miles from anywhere. It would be one hell of a journey getting there.

Maggie reappeared about an hour later. She was calm. Yet his heart sank. He knew what that peculiar calmness could mean.

'I've made up my mind, Willie. I'll have to go and see her. I'll go by boat. I don't trust aeroplanes.'

'Nobody goes by boat to America nooadays.'

'Then I'll just have to go on an aeroplane, even if it blows up. Don't try to stop me.'

He hated to say it but had to. 'It would cost far too much, pet.'

'What's money got to do wi' it when my sister's deeing?'

'You need money to buy air tickets. Lots of it. Thoosands of pounds.'

'You don't have to come. She's no' your sister. My sister's deeing and I've got a right to go and see her.'

'People often have rights, Maggie, but not the means to make use of them.'

'This is Tuesday. I'd better leave by Friday at the latest.'

In Maggie's world there were no such things as passports and visas.

'Will you see to it, Willie? If you don't want to, if you're still keeping up your spite against my sister just say so and I'll manage on my ain.'

For God's sake, Maggie, when did I ever have a spite against Elspeth? Surely it was the other way round. And, Maggie, you can hardly cross the street on your own.

He would have to find some merciful way of convincing her that it was impossible for them to raise so much money. A letter would have to do instead. He would help her to write it.

'I'll look into it, Maggie.'

4

That afternoon the debate in the Arms was on the Pope's custom of kissing the ground or rather the concrete runway of every country he visited. Charlie thought it a showman's trick for the sake of the TVcameras, while Alec was of the opinion that it set a bad example, from the hygienic point of view. To Angus it was a noble act of humility on the part of the head of the most powerful Church on earth. He looked to Willie for support, because Willie often maintained that humbleness, in persons and nations, won more respect and success than arrogance. But today Willie sat in silence, now and then shaking his head, and putting down winning dominoes without zest.

They jaloused it must be Maggie again. She was poor Willie's lifelong burden. Many a man would have fled from her long ago or if he stayed would have strangled her. Willie, though, had put up with her exasperating moods nobly and had never been heard to find fault with her.

'How's Maggie keeping these days, Willie?' asked Alec. 'Sadie was saying she met her in the street the ither day and thought she looked pale and tired.' Sadie had also said that she had looked wandered. 'She needs a holiday, Sadie thinks. Somewhere sunny. Like Spain.'

'Or California,' said Charlie. 'They say it's got the best climate in the world. There's a toon yonder, Palm Springs it's ca'd, where you get fined on the spot if you drap so much as a cigarette packet on the street. That's what I ca' civilisation.'

California, Willie remembered, was next to Arizona.

'Lots of people think America's always sunny,' said Alec, 'because of the films they see, but there are pairts where in winter the snaw's six feet high.'

'And there are tornadoes and hurricanes,' said Charlie, 'that sweep the streets faster than a million brushes.' He laughed. 'Some streets in Glesca could dae wi' a hurricane blawing doon them.'

'You're saying nothing, Willie,' said Angus. 'Has Maggie taken a bad turn?'

They knew about Maggie's weak heart.

If he told them Charlie would tell his old cat which would keep it to itself, but Angus and Alec would tell their wives who would tell other women who in their turn would pass it on until the whole district knew. If there was one thing Willie hated it was to be the subject of gossip.

But these men were his friends and he needed to confide in someone.

'Well, it is Maggie, in a way,' he said.

They waited, dominoes in their hands.

'It's really her sister, Elspeth.'

'She's the one went to America years ago?' said Alec, whose Sadie had once described Elspeth McCrae as a haughty big bitch.

Willie nodded. 'She's been in America noo for almost forty years. She used to write to Maggie fairly often but no' recently. You ken how it is. People stop writing. To tell the truth it's been years and years since Elspeth last wrote.'

'She'll be a Yank noo,' said Charlie.

'Aye. Well, Maggie got a letter this morning, no' from Elspeth hersel' but from her man, though we didn't ken she was married. It was to tell us that Elspeth's deeing of cancer.'

A coven of cardinals could not have been more solemn then. Angus was about to cross himself but with his hand at his brow remembered he was in the presence of free-thinkers; so he just scratched his brow and sighed.

Charlie frowned. For some time he had been suffering a sharp pain when pissing and was afraid it might be the beginnings of cancer. He had told no one but his cat.

Alec's mother had died, painfully, of cancer. It had been twenty years ago but tears came freshly to his eyes.

'Sad news, Willie,' said Charlie.

'Especially for Maggie,' said Angus.

'How old is she, this Elspeth?' asked Alec.

'About sixty-two.'

'That's not so very auld these days,' said Charlie.

'One thing,' said Angus, 'she'll get the best treatment over there.'

'If she can afford it,' said Alec.

'So let's hope the man she married is rich,' said Angus. 'Is he rich, Willie?'

'I don't think so. Maggie wants to go and see her before she dees.'

Again the cardinals convened. Gravely they made calculations, moral and financial. It was right and proper that Maggie should see her dying sister, but Willie's two pensions wouldn't amount to more than eighty pounds a week. Being a thrifty wee man with modest wants he had probably managed to save a little, but travelling to America would be far too expensive for him. Luckily, his Maggie was like a wean in many ways and the weans of the poor could be made to understand that many things they wanted were just not affordable. They remembered their own childhood tears of resignation.

'Whereaboots in America?' asked Alec.

'Arizona.'

'Cowboy country,' said Charlie.

'You'd think it would be healthy there,' said Angus.

'Did she marry a cowboy?' asked Charlie.

'It seems,' said Willie, diffidently,for he knew they were going to be dumbfounded, 'that she's in charge of a Christian mission.'

They were dumbfounded all right.

'Is she a minister then?' asked Charlie. 'I ken they have women ministers in America.'

'And the Pope doesn't like it,' said Alec. 'Isn't that so, Angus?'

'His Holiness is concerned only with the Catholic Church,' said Angus. 'I don't think the lady in question is a Catholic.'

'No, she isn't,' said Willie. 'She belongs to some Apostolic Church.'

'Why is it her in charge of the mission and no' her man?' asked Charlie.

'He didn't say.'

'If she's as religious as a' that,' said Alec, 'how is it she's got cancer? You'd think God would show mair gratitude.'

Those remarks were addressed to Angus who not being able to refute them, scratched his brow again and said nothing.

Willie then dropped his second bombshell. 'It's on an Indian reservation. Navajos.'

He pronounced the 'j' like a 'j'. He did not know it should have been pronounced like an 'h'.

Once again the cardinals went into session, looking perplexed.

'Indians?' said Alec at last, putting up his hand to make sure his scalp was still intact. 'The kind wi' tomahawks?'

'That live in wigwams?' said Angus.

Willie nodded, though he was sure tomahawks and wigwams were out of date.

Just then someone came into the pub and approached them. It was Duncan Forsyth. They saw that there was something wrong. But he was a man with all the cards stacked against him, who asked for nothing from anybody, who as far as they knew had no home and didn't have even a dog or cat to love him, how could there be anything more wrong with him than usual? But they saw that there was.

He did not sit down but stood beside them. He was wearing the same old raincoat and off him came the same sad smell.

'Take a seat, Duncan,' said Willie.

He shook his head. 'I just came to say goodbye.'

They were all taken aback.

'Goodbye?' said Charlie. 'Why? Where are you going?'

He gave them the most unhappy smile they had ever seen, put his hand on Willie's shoulder, and crept away.

They noticed how down at heel his shoes were, how muddy the bottoms of his trousers, and how infinitely weary his feet. At the door he turned and looked back. There was some kind of appeal on his face. Before they could call out and ask if they could help he was gone, for good this time they knew.

They stared at one another in silence. They were thanking one another for their company and friendship. They weren't outcasts, like poor Duncan.

'Maybe he's got cancer too,' said Charlie, 'and has gone somewhere to dee.'

'Elephants hae sacred places where they go to dee,' said Alec.

None rebuked him for that irrelevancy. They didn't think it irrelevant.

'If it was my last days,' said Angus, 'I'd go to Barra where it's beautiful and peaceful.'

'If you had as much money in your pockets as him,' said Charlie, 'you'd have to swim.'

'We shouldn't have let him go like that,' said Willie. 'We should have run after him and brought him back and offered oor help.'

'He made it gey clear that naebody could help him.'

'Still, Alec, we should have offered.'

Charlie was looking ashamed. 'I should have invited him to come hame with me.'

'You invited him once before, Charlie, and he just shook his heid.'

'I didn't ask seriously enough, Willie. I asked as if I didn't want him to take me at my word, and God help me neither I did.'

They stared gloomily at their empty glasses.

Alec said what they were all thinking. 'We'll be reading in the paper aboot him being found deid somewhere.'

'Dragged oot o' the Clyde,' muttered Charlie.

'Or found frozen stiff on the steps of a church,' said Angus.

'Come off it, Angus,' said Alec. 'He's no' a new-born baby. What good would he think a church would do him?'

'Maybe he'd think they could pray for his soul.'

'And what good would *that* do him?'

Immense good, thought Angus, but didn't dare say it.

'Maybe we're being too pessimistic,' said Willie. 'He could have meant he was going to some other pairt of the country where he's got relations.'

They nodded but none of them believed it.

'Pray for him, Angus,' said Alec.

He didn't know himself whether or not he was being sarcastic. Angus wasn't sure either.

Willie rose. 'I'll have to be getting hame. Maggie needs me.'

'Tell her we're very sorry to hear aboot her sister.'

'Thanks, Charlie. I'll tell her.'

'Maybe she'll get better news the next letter.'

'I hope so, Alec.'

'There are sich things as miracles,' said Angus.

'There are sich things as winning the pools,' said Charlie.

'She'll understand, Willie, that it's impossible for you to pay her fare. If we could help we would but we're a' poor men.'

'I ken that, Alec. Thanks a' the same.'

5

Willie arrived home panting. He had hurried all the way and at the end had run up the stairs. He was alarmed to find Maggie with her suitcase open on the bed. She was putting clothes into it, neatly folding every article. He had to say something to stop her and he had to say it in such a way as not to cause her grief, but were there any such words in the language?

'Are you no' being a wee bit hasty, hen?'

'She could be deid before I get there if I don't hurry.'

'She'll hang on for a while yet. Elspeth was always a brave fighter.'

'She was afraid of nothing.'

True, but he remembered it more as aggression than courage. It might be different now.

'Did I tell you, Willie, how she saved me from a big dog?'

She had told him many times.

'A big Alsatian, growling and showing its teeth. She faced up to it and stared it oot. She was just eight at the time.'

At eighteen Elspeth would have outstared a tiger. But at sixty-two there was no outstaring cancer.

Maggie held up a woollen jumper. 'Will I need this? Will it be warm or cauld there at this time of year?'

'Warm during the day I would think but cauld at night. It's in the desert, you see.'

'So I'd better take this then.'

In a drawer she came upon a small photograph. She took it out and gazed at it.

He knew that it was of her and Elspeth as children. It showed the two girls, one about six and the other about eleven. Elspeth even then was as tall as Maggie and ten times bolder. Her mouth was firm, her smile scornful, and her fists clenched. Maggie looked apprehensive, as if waiting for the camera to explode. She had never lost that look all her life.

She put the photograph in the suitcase. 'I used to have lots o' photies o' me and Elspeth. I don't ken what happened to them.' She looked at him accusingly. 'Somebody must have taken them.'

'Well, it wasn't me.'

'Trust naebody,' she muttered, and continued with her packing.

It would have been foolish to feel angry with her, but he did feel hurt. He had been married to her for over forty years and she still at times regarded him as a stranger or even an enemy. Not for the first time he wondered what his life would have been like if he had married some other woman, such as Mary Galbraith, who had been in his class at school and whom he remembered as always laughing. She had made jokes about wee Willie's wee willie. He had no idea what had become of her.

But these regrets were disloyal to Maggie and he crushed them as he had crushed them before. Who was he to think that she wasn't worthy of him? She was just as entitled to think that she could have done better than a hospital porter with a pug nose.

As considerately as he could he should be explaining to her that it was no use her packing her case, but he did not have the heart. He could only stand and watch. When she was finished he made to lift the case off the bed for her but she pushed him away. She struggled with it herself. She turned pale and gasped.

'For God's sake, Maggie,' he said.

'I don't need your help, Willie Hogg. You come in here, with the smell of drink aff your breath and tell me I need be in nae hurry to go and see my sister who's dying of cancer in a foreign land. Why should I let you help me?'

'Because I love you, hen.'

But was that true? Was it not just fondness he felt, with pity thrown in?

'What's love got to dae wi' it?' she asked, with a bitterness and relevancy that made him realise he was once again underestimating her.

'It's money that counts. Get me the money to go and see my sister. Then I'll believe you love me.'

He could have wept. This news of Elspeth had been too much for her. Many years ago a doctor had warned him that she could end up in a mental home. Thanks largely to him she had stayed just sane enough. He thought he could claim that credit.

That night, lying beside her, he wondered if it would be worthwhile going tomorrow to a travel agent and finding out just how much it would cost for the two of them to travel to Arizona. That it would be a sum far beyond their means he had no doubt, but it would be evidence that poor Maggie would have to heed.

Before falling asleep he thought of Duncan Forsyth who had no one to care for, not even an old woman with the mind of a child.

6

Next morning while Maggie was still in bed he put on the dark grey suit that he kept for Sundays and funerals and a clean shirt with a tie. He did it furtively for he was supposed to be going as usual for milk, morning rolls, and the newspaper. If Maggie had asked why he was wearing his good clothes he would have had to tell her some lie. He could hardly tell her that he might, just might, go into a travel agent's, where he would hardly be taken for a serious enquirer if he was wearing his week-day suit, baggy at the knees, and his tartan muffler. She did not ask, but as he went down the stairs he wondered if she had noticed and for her own reasons had said nothing. Children often had a cunning or instinct that prevented them from being deceived. So had Maggie.

If she wasn't curious, others were. The newsagent, Mrs Crawford, wanted to know who was dead this time and the woman in the dairy, Lizzie, said he was looking very smart for a quarter to nine on a Wednesday morning. Embarrassed, he was out of the shop before he realised that a traveller bound for Arizona would hardly go into a travel agent's with milk and rolls in one hand and the *Daily Chronicle* in the other. He couldn't take them up to the house for this time Maggie was sure to speir, nor could he ask some neighbour's wean to do it for him, for they were all on their way to school. So he had to go back into the dairy and ask Lizzie to keep them for him, as he had some business to attend to.

Not bothering to disguise her surprise and concern, (for what business could wee Willie Hogg have at that time of morning?) Lizzie asked if Maggie was all right. She hinted that he might be going for a doctor. Maggie was fine, he replied.

'She should take care, Mr Hogg.'

'I keep telling her that, Lizzie.'

'She's no' content to take her ain turn washing the stairs, she takes ither women's turns too. Did you know that, Mr Hogg?'

Aye, he knew it. Those other women didn't wash the stairs well enough to please Maggie, so she did it again after them. It had caused dissension.

About fifty yards from the travel agent's he stopped and looked into the window of a shop that sold carpets. Maggie had remarked a few days ago that they could be doing with a new fireside rug. He had promised they would get one, though he saw nothing wrong with the one they had.

The anxious, too anxious, too bloody perpetually anxious face reflected in the window suddenly annoyed him. For God's sake, all he was going to do was ask a few sensible questions about the cost of a journey. That was what travel agents were for. That was their business. They expected to be asked such questions. They had books and time-tables that contained the answers. Like every other shopkeeper with something to sell they would get more enquirers than buyers. If he went into this carpet shop he could ask them to show him a dozen rugs and in the end he could leave without buying one. They might under their breath damn him for a fussy old nuisance but to his face they would be polite. It would be the same in the travel agent's.

There were three clerks, one man and two women. Only the man was busy. He was attending to an old woman who was arranging a flight to Toronto where she was going to spend Christmas with her daughter and grandchildren. Excitement had her ready to spill out her whole life story. She was a warning to Willie. He must keep calm.

He approached the desk where a young girl with fair hair was manicuring her nails. According to a little plaque her name was Alison McLeod. She looked up with a smile made bright by the vividness of her lipstick, not, he feared, by her eagerness to oblige him.

'Can I help you?' she asked.

He sat down. If she suspected he was a fraud, wasting her time, he could hardly blame her, for that was really what he was. He and Maggie had exactly eighty-seven pounds and sixty-five pence in the building society. This journey to Arizona would cost at least a thousand pounds. So he was proposing to buy something he didn't have the money to pay for.

She was still smiling brightly. Was there in her smile a trace of impatience at this old fool who had forgotten what he had come in for?

'I'd like to find out what it would cost me and my wife to fly to a place ca'd Holbrook. It's in America, in Arizona.'

She couldn't have looked more surprised if he had said Timbuktu. 'Holbrook, Arizona?'

'The nearest big toon's Phoenix.' So the atlas had informed him.

'Ah, Phoenix, Well, well. That's far enough away. Do you know anyone there?'

'My wife's sister.'

'I see. But you've never been there before?'

'That's right.'

'May I have your name, sir?'

'Hogg, William Hogg.'

'Well, Mr Hogg, I don't think it's possible to fly straight from

Prestwick to Phoenix. You'd have to change at New York or Boston.'
She was now looking at a map of America. 'From Phoenix you should
be able to fly to Holbrook but I'd have to find out about that. Or you
could go by bus.'

He almost said that the bus would be cheaper.

He noticed the young man, probably the manager, giving him some
queer looks.

Mrs McLeod – she was wearing a wedding ring – was now consult-
ing a book with hundreds of pages. 'You want to know the cost?'

'That's right.'

'For two?'

'Aye.'

'When do you propose to make the journey, Mr Hogg?'

'As soon as possible. It's an emergency.'

'So it might have to be by scheduled flight?'

'I expect so.'

'That's a great deal more expensive.'

She was making calculations on a piece of paper.

'All in,' she said, 'for two adults, economy class, it would cost nine
hundred and fifty pounds. That's just from Prestwick to Phoenix.
From Phoenix to Holbrook would cost about two hundred pounds,
but I would have to verify that.'

'That'd be £1150 in all?' He was surprised at how quickly he had
counted it. At school he had been a dunce at mental arithmetic.

'Approximately. But of course there would be other expenses, like
hotels.'

He rose and picked up his cap. 'Thanks very much. My wife and I
will talk it over. Thanks for the trouble you've taken.'

'If you cared to call in tomorrow, Mr Hogg, I could let you have
exact figures and times.'

'Thanks.'

On the pavement outside he looked in to see if all of them, the old
woman included, were having a laugh at his expense. They were not.
Mrs Mcleod was tapping her teeth with her pen and looking pensive.
An intelligent, good-hearted girl, she had realised that the journey
must be important to him but he couldn't afford it and she felt sorry,
not because she had lost commission but because he and his wife
would be disappointed.

7

When he got home, with the rolls, milk, and newspaper, Maggie was sewing a button on to one of his shirts: an odd occupation before breakfast.

The table was set.

She made no comment on his wearing his Sunday suit.

'There's a lot of things I'll have to see to before I leave.'

If she went by herself it would halve the cost but still be far too much. Besides, how could she travel all that way by herself? Half a mile from home she got lost.

He sat down beside her. 'We've got to have a serious talk, Maggie.'

She said nothing. She concentrated on her sewing.

'I've just been to a travel agent, the people who arrange journeys and tell how much they cost.'

Still she would not look at him. Her needle, though, paused.

'The total cost would be aboot twelve hundred pounds if we baith were to go, half that if just one of us went.'

She went on with her sewing.

'Such a sum, Maggie, is away oot o' oor reach. Even if we were to sell everything we possess we would never get near it. Nae bank would lend it to us. It's a great pity but we'll just hae to write a letter. I'll help you write it, hen.'

Without a word she put down his shirt, rose, and went into the bedroom. On her face was desolation.

Christ, he thought, invoking a divinity he did not believe in. Be fair, Maggie. Don't blame me. I was only a hospital porter. I never made big money all my life. You knew that when you married me. I'd steal to get it for you but I'd just land in jail. There are moneylenders but they wouldn't lend to a couple of pensioners living in a council flat. You're in there, Maggie, breaking your heart and blaming me. I have to say it's not fair.

He went to the door of the bedroom. There was no lock or snib but he wouldn't go in without being given leave. 'Maggie, come and take your breakfast. I've made the tea.'

There was no answer.

Your sister, he said, to himself, couldn't be bothered sending you as much as a postcard these past thirty years. It wasn't her that wrote

that letter to you, but her man. He said he'd written it without her
knowledge, meaning that if she had known she would have forbidden
him. It's sad that she's so ill but don't let it come between us. Don't
let it drive you, and me with you, into that mental home.

Still she did not open the door.

He went and sat by the electric fire and spent the ten most miserable
minutes of his life, worse even than those in Africa when a shell killed
two of his mates and tore the legs off another. He had been frightened
then as well as miserable and he was frightened now too. What was
worse, being killed or having your legs torn off or losing your mind?
He imagined Maggie in the mental home, speaking to no one.

The door opened. She was dressed for outdoors, with her hat on,
and she was carrying the suitcase.

He went over to her. 'Where do you think you're going, hen?'

'Don't hen me. I'm leaving you, Willie Hogg.'

'All right, if that's whit you want. But wait for a day or two. Think
it ower. At least have your breakfast first.'

'Don't talk to me as if I was a wean.'

'But where can you go?'

They had neighbours who would take her in but only for an hour
or two. They knew the trouble he had with her but they didn't like
interfering.

'To my sister. That's where I can go.'

'But she's thoosands of miles away. You just cannae jump on a bus.'

'Laugh at me if you like but that's where I'm going. Elspeth will no'
laugh at me.'

Elspeth will ask why you came. She doesn't want you. She hasn't
for the past thirty years and now less than ever.

She began to cry, like a child. His blood froze. He could scarcely
breathe. He felt as if he was in a straitjacket, and so he was, the
straitjacket of poverty. He caught sight of a big headline in the
newspaper, about people fleeing from communism to freedom. Good
luck to them, but they'd soon find that if they didn't have money there
would be many restrictions on that freedom.

She let herself be comforted. He helped her off with her coat and
hat. He put the suitcase back in the bedroom. Then he poured her a
cup of tea. His hands shook. She wept and said she was a stupid
ungrateful old woman who didn't deserve such a good husband. She

knew they couldn't afford all that money. He had worked hard all his life and even if he had been teetotal the cost of all the beer he had drunk wouldn't have amounted to a thousand pounds, would it?

Well, would it? Say he'd drunk two pints a week for the past fifty years. Roughly speaking, that would be about five thousand pints. The price of a pint today was £1, fifty years ago it must have been a lot less. So it was quite possible that if he had been teetotal he could have saved a thousand pounds, but wouldn't he have spent it on something else?

8

Charlie McCann was to show that his resemblance to Gorbachev wasn't limited to those blemishes on his scalp. He first disclosed his brilliant plan to Polly his cat. People were generous, Glasgow people in particular, and they liked to do good turns. Willie Hogg was a popular little man. If a fund was got up to raise money to enable him and Maggie to go to Arizona to see her sister before she died the response would not be stingy. The cat miaowed agreement. Though half-blind and at twelve the equivalent of a human eighty-four she still enjoyed life thanks not only to her master's benevolence but also to the neighbours', who saved fish heads and offal for her. Boys who stoned other cats spared old Charlie's.

Every shop in the district, especially the pubs, could have a jar on the counter for contributions. Willie's old trade union could be approached for a donation. An appeal could be made from the pulpits of local churches. Neither Charlie nor Willie ever stepped inside their doors but that wouldn't matter: Christians weren't supposed to bear grudges. In any case Maggie was known to creep in now and then and sit like a mouse at the back.

It was, in a way, Polly who gave Charlie his second inspiration. Since his room-and-kitchen was two storeys up, a litter box was provided for her, lined with newspaper. It was while watching her use this, delicately, that the idea came to Charlie. Why not get a newspaper, such as the *Daily Chronicle*, which most Glasgow people read, to give the Fund some publicity? It was the kind of human story they were always looking for. Willie Hogg, war-hero. (Some exaggeration was permissible.) Ex-hospital porter. Liked by everybody who knew him.

Devoted to his wife, a woman who would have tried the patience of a saint. (Better though not to mention that.) Then there was the long-lost sister dying of cancer. Cancer was always a great help to any charitable fund-raising. But best of all – here Charlie rubbed his hands in glee – she was in charge of a Christian mission on an Indian reservation in the wilds of Arizona. God, he couldn't have invented a better story. He saw Willie and Maggie being able to travel first-class, with free champagne all the way.

There was one small snag. It was called Willie Hogg. He was a proud wee bugger who could be very thrawn if he thought his principles were being compromised. He might object to his and his wife's troubles being made public property. Still, he was loyal to Maggie and if she jumped into the Clyde he would dive in and try to save her, even if he wasn't much of a swimmer. Well, this was a different kind of dive, that was all. It could be pointed out to him, discreetly of course, that his wife's reason, not all that firmly nailed down, might become un-hinged if she wasn't allowed to go and see her sister. He didn't believe in killing his fellow man, but he had set aside his objections for his country's sake. Surely for his wife's sake he could make a similar sacrifice.

Like an unselfish statesman prepared to travel far and wide to advocate his policies, Charlie did what he would never have done on his own behalf. He went to their homes to consult Alec and Angus, risking the ire of their wives at seeing such a scruffy old scarecrow at their doors. He was not invited in, and both Alec and Angus, con-scious of their wives simmering in the background, did not give his scheme the consideration it deserved but hurriedly promised to think about it and help him put it to Willie tomorrow in the Arms.

9

Willie wasn't keen to keep his usual Thursday tryst at the pub but Maggie, undergoing one of her fits of contrition, insisted. She knew how he looked forward to his blethers with his friends. She didn't think much of his friends herself, especially Mr McCann, 'a smelly old baboon', but that didn't concern her so long as he didn't bring them home. Willie said nothing, though he was saddened by her miscalling of Charlie. They had seen baboons on television a few weeks back and

Maggie had been disgusted by their pink behinds and their habit of scratching their genitals. Charlie wasn't nearly as bad as that.

It was wet and cold that afternoon. Angus might not be present, for though inclined to fat he had a weak chest and his wife often kept him indoors. But he was there all right, with Alec and Charlie.

As they shuffled the dominoes they talked about Duncan. They reminded themselves that in the past he had disappeared for months, but this time they all felt in their bones that they would never see again that big safety-pin that substituted for the third button from the top in Duncan's raincoat.

Charlie suddenly changed the subject. 'Willie, we've got a proposition to put to you.'

Willie smiled. Charlie was a great man for propositions. 'Do you ken somebody that wants to sell a half-interest in a three-legged greyhound?'

'I'm serious, Willie. How serious are you and Maggie aboot wanting to go and see her sister that's deeing o' cancer?'

Pete Shivas, the barman, frowned and shook his head. There were certain words he did not like to hear in his pub: fuck was one, cancer another.

'Is it something, Willie,' said Alec, 'that you'd sacrifice a lot for?'

'I don't ken what you're talking aboot,' said Willie. 'Of course me and Maggie are serious aboot wanting to go, but we ken it's impossible. I went to a travel agent's and found oot the cost. Well over a thoosand pounds. So Maggie and me hae given up thinking aboot it. We're going to write a letter instead.'

'But if somebody put the money in your hand you'd go?' said Charlie, grinning like, well, like a baboon.

'Who's this philanthropist?' asked Willie, grinning himself.

'The whole city, Willie.' said Charlie. 'A public subscription.'

Willie, having no threes or twos in his hand, had to chap. He chapped. 'A public subscription? Whit are you havering aboot, Charlie?'

'The Willie Hogg Travel Fund. They'd knock each ither doon in the rush to contribute. Even the weans would bring their pennies.'

'Whit Charlie means,' said Alec, 'is that we pass roon' the hat, so to speak.'

'No!' Willie banged the table with a domino. He had turned pale.

'Haud your horses,' said Charlie. 'Alec has put it a bit crudely. Whit we're proposing, Willie, is for a jar to be put on the coonter of every shop in the district, especially the pubs.'

'You're welcome to put one on my bar,' said Peter. 'It'd soon get filled. Boozers are big-hearted.'

'A' the jars would be filled in nae time,' said Charlie. 'There's no' a better liked man in the district than Willie Hogg.'

'And hardly a worse liked one than Maggie,' thought Alec and Angus, but they didn't say it. It wasn't poor Maggie's fault that she was tuppence off the shilling.

'We're thinking of getting some publicity,' said Charlie. 'This is the sort o' story that a paper like the *Daily Chronicle* likes. If your sister-in-law had been deeing in a hospital in New York nobody would be interested, but she's running a mission, for God's sake, among heathen Indians in the wilds of Arizona. It strikes the imagination, that.'

'Donations would come flooding in from a' ower the city,' said Alec.

'Just a minute,' said Willie. 'You tell me to haud my horses, Charlie. It seems to me yours are galloping awa' with you. I'm no' making a public spectacle of myself and my wife just to gie the *Daily Chronicle* a story.'

'It wouldn't be like that, Willie. Naebody would think bad of you. The very opposite. They'd ken you were daeing it for your wife's sake. And remember this, you'd be gieing folk a chance to show how generous they are. Folk like that, Willie.'

'Don't think of yourself, Willie,' said Alec, sternly. 'Think of Maggie. It's her sister that's deeing.'

Willie was silent. In Africa once he had been on a lorry dashing across the desert with shells and bombs dropping all round. He had been terrified, but not so much as he was now, in this corner of the quiet pub, with only the clack of dominoes and the whistling breath of these old men, his friends, to be heard. More than he had ever feared death he feared making a public fool of himself and having everyone think of him as a crafty scrounger. But there was Maggie to consider. He remembered her yesterday crying like a child and him not able to comfort her. Surely if there was a chance to get her what she wanted so much he ought to seize it whatever the cost to himself?

His friends were giving him time and peace to think it over. They put the dominoes down softly. They drank their beer in respectful sips.

'A' right,' he said at last, with a heavy sigh, 'if it can be done withoot too much bally-hoo.'

They saw the tears in his eyes but pretended not to.

'On one condition.'

'Whit's that, Willie?' asked Charlie.

'Maggie's not to be involved in ony way.'

They nodded. That was easy to agree to. Maggie was best kept well in the background.

'Whit would you say,' asked Alec, 'to a wee dram to inaugurate the Willie Hogg Travel Fund?'

'Unfortunately I've left my cheque book at hame,' said Charlie.

'They're on me,' said Alec, rising and limping to the bar.

None demurred. After all, he had the biggest pension.

'Excuse me,' muttered Willie. He got up to go to the gents'.

There it occurred to him that he ought to have consulted Maggie before agreeing. She had accused him of treating her like a child. So he did, far too often. Perhaps it was the reason why she had remained like a child.

His friends were waiting for him with the whiskies set out for the toast.

'I think I ought to talk to Maggie aboot it first,' he said.

They looked at one another. He understood. They were thinking that he might as well talk to a flock of starlings.

'She has a right,' he said.

They nodded. So she had. So had the starlings.

'I think she'll agree, but she should be given her place.'

'So she should,' said Charlie, who then offered the toast. 'To the Willie Hogg Travel Fund.'

'To the Fund,' said Alec and Angus.

Willie managed to look grateful and shamefaced all at once.

10

It wasn't hard to get Maggie's approval. Still in the throes of contrition she said humbly: 'Whitever you say, Willie.' What *was* hard was getting her to understand what it was she was being asked to approve.

'It could be embarrassing,' he said.

'Whit could?'

'Well, strangers stopping us in the street and offering us money.'

'Why should they dae that? We're no' beggars.'

'It would be to help pay for oor fares to America to see Elspeth.'

'Why should they dae that? It's nane of their business.'

Well, was it? What was it somebody had said about no man being an island, that we were all dependent on one another, whether we liked it or not?

All the same he had misgivings. Suppose the whole thing misfired. He and Maggie would have suffered the humiliation without gaining the reward.

'People like to help if they can.' he said.

'Do they, Willie? I've never noticed.'

'It would be in the paper.'

'Whit paper?'

'The *Daily Chronicle*.'

'You ken I never read the paper. Only oor horoscopes.'

'They might want a picture of us.' He added ruefully, 'There's a price for everything.'

'You get nothing for nothing.'

No philosopher ever said a truer word.

'Listen, Maggie.'

'I'm listening, Willie.'

'Do you trust me?'

'I'd trust you wi' my life, Willie.'

'You ken I would never do onything to harm you.'

'Of course I ken that.'

'Right then. This whole thing could foozle oot but we'll hae faith and gie it a try. As Charlie McCann's fond of saying, look on the bright side.'

Charlie though often said it ironically.

'I'm sorry I ca'd him a smelly old baboon, but that's whit he reminds me of.'

'Weel, lass, he hasn' got a wife like you to look after him. He used to have, fifty years ago. He still misses her, though he never talks aboot her.'

'I'm no' surprised he never married again. Whit woman would have had him?'

Did baboons, like swans, keep the same mates all their lives, and if one died did the other stay single to the end?

11

Still the master-mind, Charlie decided that the most urgent thing was to get the Fund mentioned in the newspaper. People would then understand better what the jars on the counters were for. So, having no telephone at home he went out to the nearest public one and found it in working order. He didn't realise this was a minor miracle for he so seldom telephoned. He had the number of the newspaper on a bit of paper, and four ten pence coins. He hoped they would be enough. He would be justified in claiming expenses from the Fund.

'*Daily Chronicle* office,' said a woman's brisk voice. 'Can I help you?'

'I think it's me that can help you.'

'Oh. In what way?'

'I've got a story that should interest you.'

'I see. May I ask your name, please?'

'Charlie McCann.'

'Would you like to speak to a reporter, Mr McCann?'

'If that's the procedure.'

'Just a minute, please.'

'Don't waste time, young woman. I've only got three coins left.'

As he waited, while the machine ate his money, a mongrel dog came and pissed against the kiosk. Lucky, he thought.

A hearty voice this time, a man's, a young man's. 'Bill Meiklejohn here. What can I do for you?'

Charlie knew of Bill Meiklejohn. He wrote accounts of football matches.

'I'm no' sure I can explain on the telephone. It's a bit complicated and I've only got two coins left.'

'Try, anyway. Your name's Charlie McCann, isn't it?'

'Aye.'

'What age are you, Charlie?'

'Whit's that got to dae wi' it?'

'We get a lot of funny folk phoning us, Charlie. Well, old fellow, what's your story?'

'It's like this. Willie Hogg, a freend o' mine, and his wife Maggie, have just got a letter saying her sister's deeing of cancer in America.'

'Too bad, Charlie. But it's happening all the time, isn't it? It's sad but it's hardly news.'

'Wait a minute. Willie fought in Africa during the War.'

'So did thousands of others. Still not news, I'm afraid.'

'You see, Willie and Maggie cannae afford the fare to go and see her.'

'Charlie, I'd like to spend Christmas in Barbados but I can't afford the fare.'

'Dammit, his wife's sister, the one who's got cancer, who went to America mair than thirty years ago, runs a mission on an Indian reservation in Arizona.'

There was a pause.

'Now that's more like the thing, Charlie. A religious mission?'

'Aye. Some apostolic church.'

'Red Indians?'

'Navajos, Willie said.' He pronounced the 'j' like a 'j'.

'Navajos, Charlie.' Meiklejohn pronounced the 'j' as if it was an 'h'. 'So what we have is a missionary dying of cancer on a Navajo reservation in Arizona?'

'That's right.'

'She's Scottish?'

'Born in Glesca.'

'How old is she?'

Charlie lied. 'Aboot fifty.' If he had told the truth and said about sixty Meiklejohn might have lost interest.

'There *could* be a story in this, Charlie. Mind you, just could, I'd like to come and talk to you about it. Where d'you live?'

Charlie gave his address.

'Will you be in this afternoon?'

'Aye.'

'Right. I might look in on you about three, if nothing more interesting turns up. Like a murder,' he added, cheerfully.

He was at Charlie's door at ten past three, a young man with red hair and a merry grin, wearing a sheepskin coat and blue jeans. He endeared himself to Charlie right away by patting Polly's head. What was more she liked it. It wasn't everybody that she let pat her head.

He was a man who noticed things. 'Did anybody ever tell you, Charlie, that those marks on your scalp are like the birth marks on Gorbachev's?'

'You're the ninety-ninth. The next yin gets the prize. A kick on the erse.'

Meiklejohn laughed. 'I like a man with a sense of humour. Now tell me more about this broad from Glasgow that's trying to convert the heathen Navajos.'

'Whit's a broad?'

'American for woman.'

Charlie told the story.

Meiklejohn kept nodding. 'I think I could do something with it, Charlie. Not quite front page stuff, though.'

'I've seen on your front page rubbish aboot a whure and a millionaire.'

'That was last week. But, Charlie, you shouldn't say whure. You should say call girl. Did you see the picture of her? A real smasher, with marvellous tits. She'd cost you five hundred quid a night, that one. You see, Charlie, all the men that saw it wanted to go to bed with her and all the women wanted to go to bed with the millionaire on his big yacht. That's why it was on the front page.'

'I never wanted to go to bed with her.'

Meiklejohn glanced at the portrait on the mantelpiece of a young woman with a happy smile.

'My wife,' said Charlie. 'She died fifty years ago.'

'I'm sorry to hear that, Charlie. And you never married again?'

'I never found anyone that could take her place.'

'I could believe that, Charlie. She looks as if she had the gift of happiness. Now, what's this Maggie like? The missionary's sister, I mean.'

'Well, she's nae smasher and she's no' got marvellous tits. But then she's seventy years of age or near enough.'

'Is she tragic-looking?'

'Whit do you mean?'

'Sad and sorrowful?'

'Wouldn't you be if your only sister was deeing of cancer? To tell you the truth—and I ken that's a' you fellows are after, the truth—'

'Now, Charlie, no sarcasm.'

'Maybe it would be true to say Maggie's no' quite a' there.'

'You mean?' Meiklejohn tapped his brow.

'She's not a raving lunatic, but she's a bit simple and gets wandered at times.'

'I think we'd have to leave that out. People don't find much romance in doited old women. Well, Charlie, I'll talk it over with my editor and if he thinks it worth a paragraph or two I'll be in touch with you again. I'd like to have a word with Willie Hogg. Could that be arranged?'

'Aye, but you'd have to handle him carefully.'

'Why? Don't tell me he's weak in the head too.'

'That's just whit he isnae. Maybe he's no' as quick on the uptake as myself, say, but he thinks things through and ends up wi' the richt answers.'

'Good. Where does he live?'

'I don't think you should go there. Whit aboot the *Airlie Arms*? That's oor howff.'

'In Wallace Street?'

'Aye. Do you ken it?'

'Charlie, in the course of my business I've been in every pub in the city.'

'Could you get me a job like that?'

'Our howff, you said. Who are we? Just you and this Willie Hogg?'

'And yin or twa ithers.'

'I don't want to meet them, Charlie. Just you and Willie.'

'Sure.' Come to think of it there was no need for Alec and Angus to be present. The fewer voices the better. They were good friends but they liked having their say whether it was useful or not. He had always seen the advantages of one-man rule, provided of course that one man was capable and fair-minded. 'Would the morrow suit you, Mr Meiklejohn?'

'It would. At what time?'

'Whit aboot eleven in the morning? It'll be quiet then.'

'Right, I'll be there.'

'I hope you understand that the purpose is to raise money to send Willie and Maggie to America.'

'I understand, Charlie.'

'The Willie Hogg Travel Fund.'

'It's a good idea. It's possible the paper might chip in with a tenner or two.'

'I'm expecting it to dae a lot better than that. Are no' newspapers rotten wi' money?'

Meiklejohn grinned. 'Look at all the free publicity you'll be getting.'

'When will the story appear?'

'Probably on Friday.'

On his way out Meiklejohn again patted Polly on the head and again she let him. 'I like cats,' he said. 'Oh, by the way, Charlie, ask Willie to bring his medals with him. I might have a photographer with me.'

He went off whistling.

Would Willie Hogg let himself be photographed wearing his medals for a picture to appear in a newspaper?

When whisky was free.

12

The Gorbachev of the Cowcaddens, alias Charlie McCann, having confirmed his own decision that there was no need for a meeting of the whole Polit Buro, sent one summons only. It was to Willie. In his note, delivered by a neighbour's wean, Charlie suggested that Willie should bring his medals, in his pocket, just in case; but he was sure Willie would do no such thing.

Charlie arrived first at the *Arms*, soon after the doors opened. He was swithering whether to order or to wait for Meiklejohn and let him order when Willie came in, wearing not medals but an anguished face. Now, thought Charlie, if it was me that was going to be famous I would be grinning gallusly, to show the bastards what I really thought of them. But then I was never as nice a man as Willie. I've never trusted my fellow man as he's done and I was never liked as much. The funny thing is I've always been more of an optimist than him. That could be because I've never had as high an opinion of my fellow man. If the whole human race blew itself up I wouldn't be surprised and I wouldn't be heart-broken either, whereas Willie with his last gasp would be shouting what a bloody shame, it could all have been so different.

But then his wife, such as she is, poor soul, didn't die when she was twenty-five.

They sat in their usual corner.

'Alec and Angus are no' coming, Willie. It's just you and me.'

'Oh.'

'And this reporter fellow. We'll wait and let him order. It'll be the paper that'll pay. Did you bring your medals?'

'I did not. Was that a joke, Charlie?'

'It was the reporter suggested it.'

'If I've to have my photie in the paper wearing medals the whole thing's aff.'

'Why, Willie? Are you ashamed o' them?'

'No, but I'm no' prood o' them either.'

'But you won them fair and square. You didn't buy them frae a pawnshop.'

'No, but they were just routine issue. You got them for just being there.'

'Wasn't being there enough?' Charlie himself had missed active service because of a gammy leg that had never troubled him since.

'In war, Charlie, atrocious things are done by baith sides. We a' share the blame.'

He didn't mention that Maggie often took out his medals and polished them.

Just then, Meiklejohn sauntered in, accompanied by another man, carrying a camera.

Pete Shivas, the barman, knew why they were there. He eyed them speculatively. Could he interest them in the fate of the *Arms*, soon to be demolished? An article in the paper could attract a shoal of customers in its last days.

Charlie introduced Meiklejohn to Willie. The reporter looked relieved. Hogg could easily have been a dead loss as far as human interest went. The world was full of such dead losses, as every reporter knew, but here, even without medals, was a wee man who represented a number of Glasgow virtues, such as decency, modesty, and humour, with a dash of thrawnness.

Willie took some convincing that a photograph was necessary. Did he mind it being mentioned that he had served in North Africa and fought against Rommel? No, but he doubted very much if Rommel had ever heard of him. What kind of woman was Elspeth? Surely she must be courageous, enterprising, and self-sacrificing? He didn't know about courageous: Indians didn't go on the warpath these days. Did he know the name of the reservation? Yes, he did. It was called Broken Arrow. Meiklejohn was delighted. If he had made it up and he had been prepared to make it up, he couldn't have done better. What about Mrs Hogg? He'd rather Maggie was left out of it. She was upset enough because of her sister's illness.

The story would probably appear tomorrow, said Meiklejohn. The Fund would be mentioned but no direct appeal for contributions would be made. There could be legal obstacles. But the paper would make a donation. Charlie said he hoped it would be a big one.

Before leaving Meiklejohn ordered two more pints for the old men.

Charlie was satisfied, like a statesman who had just concluded an advantageous treaty. 'You're as guid as on that plane, Willie.'

13

The article took up half an inside page, with a big black headline – GLASGOW WOMAN DYING AMONG REDSKINS – and there was a photograph of Willie, making him look, as he muttered to himself, a right gomeril. But Mrs Crawford, the newsagent, thought it a good likeness of him, and so did the three customers in the shop at the time. Indeed, they all gazed at him with a new respect. He thought at first it was because he had subdued his pride for his wife's sake but soon realised that had nothing to do with it, he had simply got his picture in the paper without having had to commit rape or murder to earn the honour.

People stopped him in the street to congratulate him. Though Glasgow Rangers had just signed an English player for half a million pounds it was wee Willie Hogg that most Glasgow households talked about that morning. In a few he was sourly censured as a publicity-seeker, and in one or two suspected of being a con-man. But nearly everybody wished him and Maggie well. As Charlie McCann had prophesised people were eager to help so deserving and so unusual a cause. Though no direct appeal had been made the *Chronicle* received an avalanche of envelopes inscribed The Willie Hogg Travel Fund and containing sums from twenty pounds to ten pence. The paper proudly announced it was contributing five hundred pounds.

Charlie was gleeful. He had been round the shops. The jars were filling up, not only with coins but with notes too. They were to remain on the counters for a fortnight. Any longer and Elspeth might be dead but even then, as Charlie pointed out, the money could be used to fly Willie and Maggie to America for the funeral.

But by the end of the fortnight Charlie had been deposed. A committee of responsible men took over: a councillor, a minister, and a bank manager. This, they said, the law required. No one actually accused Charlie of being in it for his cut but no one acquitted him either. He was just pushed out of the way and was very bitter. In vain he telephoned Meiklejohn. 'Sorry, Charlie. It's got too big.' For another photograph had appeared in the paper, of Willie and Maggie, with the Lord Provost.

The Fund reached the 'handsome sum' of £10321.

Willie did not think it was handsome. It was excessive. It almost had him believing that he *was* a con-man. He was vexed too that Charlie had been so unfairly treated.

He and Maggie were summoned before the committee.

It was like a Social Security tribunal investigating the possibility of fraud. The committee sat on one side of the table, Willie and Maggie on the other. The place was a small room in a church hall. It was chilly. The chairs were uncomfortable.

Willie felt that his honesty was being questioned. He was tempted to tell them to stick the money up their jumpers, but for Maggie's sake he kept his temper. Poor Maggie was confused enough without him getting into a squabble with these worthy, well-intentioned, but smug gentlemen, who were, as the councillor who was the chairman, kept saying, simply looking after the interests of the subscribers to the Fund. He was sure Mr Hogg understood.

Mr Hogg said he did. He said it grimly.

'The total sum, as you may know, Mr Hogg, now stands at £10321. It is possible some late contributions will still come in. Now, as you will be the first to agree, Mr Hogg, that is well in excess of your requirements.'

'It could be,' said Willie, 'but you never can tell.'

They looked perplexed.

'You will appreciate,' said the councillor, 'that it cannot be simply a matter of handing over the money to you.'

'Why? Are you saying I cannae be trusted?'

'It is not a matter of trust, Mr Hogg. There are legal implications. Everything must be seen to be above board. What we propose is to provide you and your wife with air-tickets from Prestwick to Holbrook, Arizona, which we have been advised is the nearest town to the mission. An adequate sum will be provided for essential expenses en route, such as hotel bills, though we may assume that you will be offered accommodation at the mission.'

'Judging by this postcard,' said the minister, with a greasy smile, 'you should be very snug there.'

The postcard was passed round. It showed, in bright colours, some white buildings amidst a large garden full of trees and flowers. This was, it said on the back, the St Aloysius Mission in Santa Barbara, California.

'Receipts would be appreciated,' said the councillor.

'If we buy cups of coffee do we ask for receipts?'

'Such small sums may be disregarded.'

'We are confident, Mr Hogg,' said the minister, with another greasy smile, 'that you and Mrs Hogg will not indulge in unseemly extravagances.'

So far the banker had said nothing. Did he now wink?

'We anticipate there will be a substantial surplus,' said the councillor. 'It will have to be decided in due course what use this should be put to.'

'Why not a Christmas party for the weans of the district?' said Willie.

The minister frowned at that frivolity.

'Couldn't it be used for Elspeth?' asked Maggie. 'To pay for her medical expenses?'

That very sensible suggestion disconcerted them, especially as it had come from such an unlikely source.

Willie was proud of her. He patted her arm.

'Will not the unfortunate lady's expenses be paid by the Mission authorities?' said the minister.

'Besides,' said the councillor, 'though our sympathies, of course, are with the lady such a purpose would be well outside the scope of the Fund, the name of which, let us keep in mind, is the William Hogg Travel Fund. It cannot therefore, legally or morally, be used for any other purpose.'

'That's right,' said Willie. 'It's got to be spent on our journey. Isn't that so? Isn't that the law?'

If they had been playing chess he would have had them check-mated.

He rubbed it in. 'It was Glasgow folk that contributed. Do you ken whit they would say? They would say, we're sorry for Maggie's sister, a Glasgow woman, dying thoosands o' miles frae hame, but here's money for you baith to go and see her before she dees and maybe comfort her. Tell her all Glasgow wishes her well. We ken, Willie, it's nae pleasure trip but make it as easy on yourselves as you can. Remember you represent us. We've got a reputation in the world for decency and generosity. Don't let us doon.'

The minister, originally from Edinburgh, was flabbergasted. 'Are you demanding, Mr Hogg, that you should have this large sum to spend as you please?'

'I'm demanding nothing. I'm just telling you whit I think maist Glasgow folk would say. We might want to buy Elspeth a few comforts. Do you think Glasgow folk would say no? We might want to gie something to the Indians. We might even when we get hame buy a new three-piece suite for oor living-room. Whitever we did we'd hae Glasgow's blessing.'

'How can you tell that?' asked the minister, peevishly.

'Because I ken them. Because I'm one of them. They're famous for their sense of humour.'

Did the banker wink again? He spoke for the first time. 'I suggest that an account be opened in Mr Hogg's name,'

'Would I have a cheque-book?' asked Willie.

'Yes, you would.'

'Ony cheque I signed I'd keep a record o' for your inspection, gentlemen.'

'Especially the one for the new three-piece suite,' said the banker, laughing.

The minister dimly saw that it was a joke. He tried to smile. 'Have you seriously considered, Mr Hogg, whether you and Mrs Hogg are able physically to undertake such a long journey? Have you consulted your doctor? I understand Mrs Hogg does not keep well.'

'I'm well enough' said Maggie.

'Thanks,' said Willie. 'Whit you're saying, in a roondaboot kind of way, is that since we're baith auld we should take great care of ourselves and never mind the expense.'

'Yes, I think that is what Mr Donaldson is saying,' said the banker, 'and I certainly endorse it.'

The councillor had to endorse it too. Perhaps, thought Willie, it had occurred to him that he might lose votes at the next election if it had got out that he had been mean, with money too that didn't belong to him.

Going home, Willie felt like dancing a jig on the pavement, but walked sedately beside Maggie who clung to his arm.

'You shouldn't have been sae cheeky to the minister, Willie,' she said.

'I just told him a few home truths, that's all.'

'But we cannae buy a new three-piece suite, can we?'

'That was a joke, hen.'

And one that Glasgow would have enjoyed. Fly men, as long as they were humorous with it, added to the jolliness of life. That three-piece suite might have become famous.

'Should we go and see the doctor, Willie?'

'I think so, hen. For one thing, you'll need a supply of pills.'

'Mind you, even if he says I shouldnae go I'm still going.'

'Sure you are.' He smiled and squeezed her arm. She was all right, his Maggie.

14

Dr Saunders was big, jocular, and frank. He had won Willie's confidence by admitting that nature did most of the healing. What doctors could do was cheer up patients while nature was at work. His own patients badly needed cheering up by the time he saw them, for they had to sit for as long as an hour and a half in a dismal waiting-room with no carpet on the floor and metal-framed chairs that gave you a sore back. Good enough for the poor, Willie had thought, indignantly. Better facilities had been promised when money was available, but a lot of Dr Saunders's patients would never benefit from them, being old and infirm; as indeed most of them were on the morning that Willie and Maggie attended for Maggie's supply of pills.

One old man, Bert Yuill his name was, kept giving them long calculating glances. He was notorious in the district as an expert welfare scrounger and prodigious boozer. His nose was like a squashed tomato going bad in places, and on either side of it glittered

a small sly eye. When it was his turn to go and see the doctor he
hobbled over, helped by a stick, and said hoarsely: 'Are you that fellow
Hogg that's getting a' the money', meaning, 'Are you the swindler
that's getting away with it?' Willie felt mortified. How many in the city
were thinking that of him? It was a credit to his humanity that he felt
no satisfaction as he watched the old twister creep out of the room,
shuffling and wheezing, for he suffered from a combination of bunions and bronchitis.

'Do you ken who that was?' whispered Maggie.

'Aye. Everybody kens Bert Yuill.'

'He's living wi' a woman half his age.'

Willie hadn't known that. Yuill was at least seventy. Good luck to
him then and his thirty-five-year old paramour.

'A trollop that dyes her hair.'

How did Maggie know all this?

'Weel, as long as they're happy,' he said.

'They come hame every Saturday night, drunk.'

'Who telt you this, Maggie?'

'I ken things you don't, Willie. You're mair interested in what you
read in the paper than in the folk that live a' round you.'

Was that true? Was he more interested in the Poles, say, than in the
Scots? But then, whenever he went along to the public library for a
free read of the *Guardian* there were plenty of articles about the Poles
and damned few about the Scots.

Maggie was now whispering so quietly he could hardly hear her.
'They were seen once in their close daeing yon.'

Doing yon meant making love. He could not help grinning. Apart
from Bert's bunions and bronchitis and his lady friend's dyed hair the
stone floor of a close smelling of cats' piss was surely a purgatorial bed
on which to make love, and there was a danger of frightened cats
jumping on you and doing painful damage to intimate parts. When
you came to think of it there were tribes in Glasgow more outlandish
than any Navajos.

At last it was their turn.

The doctor was seated at his desk, with their cards in front of him.
He was as good-humoured as ever but also, Willie noticed, a bit
tired-looking. Maybe he had been called out during the night.

'Well now, the celebrated Mr and Mrs Hogg,' he said.

'So you've heard aboot the Fund, doctor?'

'I contributed to it.'

'Thanks. We've come to see if you've any advice for us and Maggie needs a fresh supply of pills.'

'I can give you the pills but I'm not so sure about the advice. If I was to say that it wasn't advisable for Mrs Hogg with her heart condition, would she stay at home?'

'No, she wouldn't,' said Maggie.

The doctor laughed. 'I thought as much.'

'Even if I was deeing I'd gang to the moon to see my sister.'

'Good for you. I believe the Fund raised a goodly sum. Use every penny of it to make your journey and your stay in America as restful and free from strain as possible.'

'Is that your professional advice, doctor?'

'It is, Mr Hogg, and you can quote me. I believe the air in Arizona's clear and healthy. A sojourn in it should do you both a lot of good. Just take it easy, especially you, Mrs Hogg. This sister of yours, she'll be getting the best of medical care, I should imagine.'

'That's not what we've been told,' said Willie. 'As a matter of fact we're no' sure that she's getting any medical care at a'.'

'What do you mean?'

'It seems she's very religious. According to her man who wrote to us she thinks it's a maitter entirely between her and God. If He doesn't want to cure her, then naebody else can.'

The doctor's smile faded. 'Well, let's hope God's kind to her.'

'He's no' been very kind to her so far,' said Maggie.

The doctor and Willie exchanged glances. Here was Maggie, the simple soul, going straight to the point.

'I hope she's not refusing to take pain-killers,' said the doctor.

'When oor Elspeth says a thing, doctor, she sticks to it.'

The doctor shook his head. 'Well, good luck to you both. When you get back be sure to come in and tell me how you got on.'

They promised and left.

15

They were to fly off early on Friday. Nevertheless, Willie kept his Thursday tryst in the *Airlie Arms*. He had missed the last four. He could have offered business as his excuse, but another reason was that he had come to hate the notoriety that the Fund had given him. He couldn't go for a loaf of bread without being stopped by some stranger wanting to shake his hand and wish him well. It was mostly kindness on their part but he soon found it unbearable. He was beginning not to know himself any longer. When he looked in the mirror he hardly knew this obnoxious old bugger with the phony smile. It was almost a relief, though a heartbreak, when, instead of being congratulated, he was cursed; as he was once, by a woman, a complete stranger, who was waiting at his closemouth one evening. She looked mad, poor soul, and sounded it too, though what she said had bitter sense. Her man had died of cancer a few weeks ago and nobody had given her anything. No fund had been set up for her and her three children. There was nothing he could say. He took out his wallet and was looking in it for a five-pound note when she struck it from his hand and rushed off weeping. In tears himself he picked up his wallet and crept into the close. There he stood with his face pressed against the cold wall, profoundly miserable.

So, on his way to the *Airlie Arms*, he skulked close to the buildings, in the shadows. His cap was pulled down over his eyes, like Duncan Forsyth's, and his raincoat collar pulled up. If a police car passed, he thought, they would take him for a would-be rapist.

Would the pub be a haven or a stormy passage? He had heard that his friends, Charlie particularly, were displeased with him for having shunned them to hobnob with important people like the Lord Provost. It was true that Charlie, whose idea it had been in the first place, had been unfairly treated, but it hadn't been Willie's fault.

They were present all right, the three of them, in their usual corner and with dominoes on the table; but their faces were glum, and to the glumness was added resentment when he joined them with his pint in his hand. It struck him that Pete the barman had been a bit curt when serving him.

'Well, how have you a' been?' he asked.

'We've been oorselves,' muttered Alec.

'No' like somebody we could name,' said Angus.

'I'm sorry I wasnae able to come before this.'

'Having tea wi' the Lord Provost, were you, Willie?' asked Charlie.

'Are you sure it wasnae wi' the Prime Minister, Charlie?' asked Alec.

Willie smiled, with some difficulty. 'If you want to ken, I've been to Edinburgh to the American consulate to get visas for me and Maggie.'

'So it was the American ambassador you had tea wi',' said Charlie. 'If this is a joke I'm no' appreciating it.'

'You've sold yourself to the enemy, Willie,' said Angus. 'That's nae joke.'

'Whit do you mean?'

'Tell him, Charlie,' said Alec.

'They've bought you, Willie,' said Charlie.

Willie grew tense. 'Who've bought me?'

'Whit you used to ca' the Establishment.'

'Aye, the Establishment,' said Angus. 'Them wi' the money.'

'Them wi' the power,' said Alec.

'In this very pub,' said Charlie, 'you've accused men like Harry Armstrong and Jimmy Heddleston of being bought by the Establishment.'

Armstrong and Heddleston were trade union leaders who had made many speeches calling for the abolition of the House of Lords and then, when they retired, had become members of it.

'You're no' comparing me wi' them, are you? For God's sake, be reasonable.'

'So it's "for God's sake", is it?' said Charlie. 'So you've joined the Kirk as weel?'

'This must be a joke and a damned stupid one at that. If you're referring to me getting my photie in the paper and being gi'en money to take my wife to see her sister in America let me remind you whose idea it was and what was my first response. I didn't want onything to do with it. You a' coaxed me. There's Pete will tell you.'

'Leave me out of it,' said Pete.

'Who telephoned the paper? Who brought the reporter to see me. You ken I only agreed for Maggie's sake.'

'You're condemning yourself oot o' your ain mooth,' said Charlie. 'Aye, it was me, Alec, and Angus who got you the publicity and started the Fund. Then whit happened? You drapped us, you stopped coming here, you went aff wi' Lord Provosts, cooncillors, and ministers, important people, solid citizens, no' scruffy auld pensioners like us. It's been done many times doon the ages but it's always a sair disappointment when a comrade goes ower to the enemy for his ain advantage. We liked you, Willie. We thought there wasnae a mair decent and loyal man in the whole of Glesca. I'm sorry to say we cannae think that noo.'

Willie saw then, with dismay, that Charlie at least was in earnest. He also saw, with pity, that Charlie himself had been hungering for some of the limelight.

'I'm sorry, Charlie,' he said, 'but I don't see whit else I could hae done. I became, you micht say, a prisoner of circumstances.'

All three attacked him then.

'You could hae withdrawn before they got their claws into you.'

'When they started praising you frae the pulpits.'

'When they photographed you wi' the Lord Provost.'

'When the Conservative candidate sent you a letter.'

'Lots of people sent me letters.'

'But you liked it, Willie. You liked being famous.'

'Famous, Charlie? How was I famous? Because a lot of people wrote me letters wishing me and my wife well didnae make me famous.'

'Did you answer those letters?' asked Alec.

'No, I didn't. Maybe I should have but I didn't. Maggie thought I should.'

'Did you feel too high and mighty to answer them'

'No, Charlie. If you want the truth, I felt too embarrassed.'

'How were you embarrassed?' asked Angus, with a sneer.

Willie let himself be provoked. 'I'll tell you how, Angus. Alang wi' one of the letters was a coloured picture. Of a saint. A Catholic saint. The woman who sent it said it would bring me good fortune if I prayed to it every day. She said I should take it to Elspeth and maybe it would cure her. That embarrassed me, Angus, a hell of a lot.'

He got up. He had hardly touched his beer. He felt as he had done in the close with his face pressed against the wall.

'Do you think they mean it?' he asked Pete at the bar.

'Aye, they mean it, Willie. They think you've let them doon.'

'I cannae see how.'

'Maybe that's the trouble.'

But as he made his way home Willie just could not see what he had done to deserve the name of traitor. It was true he must have accepted money from people whose opinions and principles he would probably have despised, but people were more than their despicable opinions and principles, they were also generous impulses, and they were vulnerable creatures liable themselves to be stricken by cancer. Was it treacherous of him to see Charlie, Alec, and Angus as disappointed jealous old men whose horizons were too narrow? He himself was ignorant and uneducated, but in the past three weeks he had learned a lot not only about himself but also about other people, including his own wife. He had been given a more hopeful, a more heart-warming, view of humanity. Why should he be ashamed of it just because his friends chose to misunderstand?

All the same he felt kinship with a stray cat that darted across his path miaowing pitifully. It was as black as the devil and had green eyes.

Part Two

1

A local taxi company had offered, as its contribution, to drive them to Prestwick Airport, gratis. The driver knocked on their door promptly at half past seven in the morning and volunteered to carry their suitcases downstairs. Willie then waited patiently while Maggie, for the third time, went about seeing to it that the gas was turned off and all the electric plugs were pulled out from the wall. Then she sat down, hat on head and handbag on her lap, and gazed round the living-room, at the photograph of her and Willie and the swans on the mantelpiece, the porcelain shepherdess beside it, the chest of drawers her grandfather, a cabinet maker, had made seventy years ago, and at her cherished picture of Mary, Queen of Scots, landing at Leith, which she had bought in an antique shop.

'You never ken, Willie,' she said, with a sigh. 'We might never see it again.'

He felt very protective. He would bring her back, safe and sound.

'That's him tooting, hen. Time to go.'

Some neighbours were at the closemouth to see them off.

'Guid luck, Willie,' they said, and added, not quite so cordially. 'Guid luck, Maggie.'

Had she noticed? He suspected she did, though she gave no sign and thanked them politely. In the past three weeks since receiving the letter he had come to realise that she had qualities hidden even from him. If he had misjudged her why should he be surprised or hurt when other people misjudged her too? He must cherish her all the more.

The driver was a good-natured but garrulous man, who thought it part of the service to keep the two poor old souls entertained, so he told them funny stories of people he had taken to airports, weddings, funerals, and once to Barlinnie Prison. Maggie escaped as usual by going off into a dwam, leaving Willie to laugh at the amiable nonsense when he felt more like crying.

He would have to keep control of himself. He was becoming a bundle of nerves. How could he look after Maggie if he himself went to pieces?

They arrived at the airport with an hour and a half to spare. The taxi-driver carried their cases to the queue at the check-in desks.

'Think you'll manage from here on?' he asked, anxiously.

'Aye, we'll manage,' said Willie. 'Thanks for a' the trouble you've taken. How much do I owe you?'

'Not a penny. It's a' on the house.'

Nevertheless Willie had a five pound note ready. He had decided to take the doctor's advice and make the journey as free of stress as possible. What better oil than money? One advantage of having plenty of it was that you could tip without worrying whether it was too much or too little.

The driver accepted it, with a wink. He knew that the Fund had amounted to thousands.

Willie felt a spasm of conscience but a glance at Maggie cured it immediately. She was looking about her so eagerly: not childish this time but child-like. People were smiling at her hat, with liking and goodwill.

There was a long slow queue waiting to check in, but only, Willie soon discovered, for those travelling economy class. He and Maggie were travelling first class.

After giving it more anguished thought than a Prime Minister about to declare war he had decided that it would be a legitimate expense. Had not the doctor advised it, and had not Mrs McLeod the young travel agent recommended it? Wasn't that what the money was for? she had asked. There would be more space and therefore less strain. They would arrive not so worn out.

All the same he felt sheepish and a wee bit guilty as he checked in at the first-class desk.

The girl there looked surprised when he and Maggie approached and was about to tell them they were in the wrong place when she glanced at their tickets. She became at once respectful and attentive but still surprised.

People in the economy class queue were eyeing him and Maggie with considerable interest, and their suitcases too, which were hardly the kind first class passengers ought to possess. Willie regretted not having bought new ones, of expensive leather. He would have been spared these amused and puzzled looks, which did upset him a little.

Were these people thinking that he and Maggie must have won the pools? Perhaps some recognised him from his picture in the paper. Were they feeling peeved that they, paying with their own money, were travelling economy class while he and Maggie, paying with other people's money, were treating themselves to first class, with free champagne and a fancier meal? But did they as taxpayers object when MPs visited foreign countries at their expense? Weren't he and Maggie Glasgow's ambassadors? In any case if they had had to stand in that long slow-moving queue they would have been tired out before they'd even seen the plane.

But he wasn't altogether reassured and kept his head down.

Maggie, though, seemed to have no such anxieties. It could have been because she wasn't fully aware of the situation but somehow he didn't think so. She was simply glad that they didn't have to stand for hours, waiting. It was the attitude of a realist. Like a good football player she was keeping her eye on the ball; which in her case was getting to Arizona to see her sister. Nothing else mattered.

If there was a departure lounge for first-class passengers Willie didn't try to find out where it was. He felt happier with people who were like Maggie and him, except that they didn't have first-class tickets. Their dress, their accents, their hand luggage, were similar to Maggie's and his, except that Maggie seemed to be the only woman in the whole airport wearing a hat. Among first-class passengers they would have looked and felt out of place. It would be different on the plane where they would be hidden except from a few.

He had expected to have to keep on encouraging Maggie, who had so often expressed a fear of flying, but no, she sat at her ease among the three hundred or so passengers, by no means the most apprehensive person there. She had sympathy for any who looked scared. 'Look at that poor soul over there, Willie, in the green coat. That's twice she's crossed herself.' When two toddlers playing with toy cars came very close to her feet she smiled and asked them their names. They trusted her immediately. One said his name was Robert, the other that she was Samantha, and then they rushed away again in pursuit of their cars. 'Nice children,' she said, when he had been half-expecting her to say, 'Little nuisances.'

When they came out on to the concourse and saw the huge plane, a Jumbo Jet, Willie felt excited and showed it, but Maggie by his side told him not to be afraid, it was safer travelling by aeroplane than by motor car.

Going up the steps behind her he noticed what he had long forgotten, how shapely her legs still were and how neat her ankles. In those long-ago days when he had courted and married her she had never been what people called good-looking, her nose was too thin for that and her chin too long, but she had had a trim figure and an unconsciously elegant walk.

Shown to her seat by the American hostess she said 'Thank you', so politely that the girl gave her the smile reserved not just for first-class passengers but only for those first-class passengers who would give her no trouble during the flight. One of Maggie's worries had about going to the toilet but in the first-class section the toilets were handily placed. She let Willie fasten her seat-belt for her though she assured him she knew how to do it. She looked about her at the other passengers. One was a woman with pearls. 'You can see they're real, Willie.' When the plane took off, while other passengers were keeping their fingers crossed, in quite a few cases literally, she looked eagerly out of the window. 'Look, Willie, mountains. Will that be Arran? Yonder's Rothesay Bay. Remember when you took us out in a rowing boat and lost an oar and a wee boy in another boat had to get it for you?'

He noticed she was speaking what she would have called proper. Had she consciously decided to do so or was it an instinctive reaction?

'It's not as noisy as I thought it would be, Willie, or as bumpy.'

When the meal came she wasn't daunted by some unusual items and ate it all. He left half of his.

Already she was proving a better traveller than he. She went to the toilet and came back comfortable. He went and came back feeling he needed to go again.

Yet he still felt he had to encourage her. 'You're daeing fine, lass,' he whispered.

She patted his hand. 'So are you, Willie, but don't look so worried.'

When other passengers in the first-class section smiled at her she just smiled back, as if it was the natural thing to do. His smiles, though, were at first clouded with inhibition.

These were all well-off people accustomed to travelling in this style: supporters of the Establishment no doubt. But they weren't his enemies even if they did have a lot more money than he, and it would be stupid to say he had gone over to them just because he was travelling in the same part of the plane. If I think I'm inferior to them then I'll feel inferior and look it too, so I'm damned if I'm going to think it. His smiles then became friendlier and more confident.

The air hostess chatted to them about the rest of their journey. She had been to Phoenix; it was a lovely city. She had never been to Holbrook, though. That was close to the Grand Canyon, did they know?

'Noo that's a place I've always wanted to see,' said Willie.

'Well, now's your chance,' said Maggie, with a smile.

'I believe you can hire a plane and fly over it,' said the hostess.

'Why don't we do that, Willie?' asked Maggie.

He had often been sad that she never seemed able to appreciate his jokes. Now he wasn't sure whether or not *she* was joking. For a few seconds he scarcely recognised her. Here was no lost, bewildered woman. Here was a woman who had discovered herself. He had been afraid that the sight of Elspeth dying might derange her. Now he saw that she would face it bravely and intelligently.

The hostess was puzzled. She still could not figure out this odd pair. They didn't look as if they had lots of money but they must have, otherwise how could they travel first class and talk about hiring a private plane? Had they robbed a bank? To an American the idea was not absurd. Not long ago in her home town a couple as ordinary as these had been found guilty of killing and burying in their backyard ten young children. In any case Mr and Mrs Hogg were passengers on her plane and must be shown respect and deference. So she told them about a magnificent new hotel in Phoenix. Film stars stayed there. The foyer was as large as a church and had in it a big golden statue of the phoenix, the mythical bird, rising from the flames.

'What's it called then, this hotel?' asked Willie.

'*The Excelsior*, sir.'

The rich never asked the price of anything, so he didn't, and Maggie, good sport, didn't either. She just said, 'It sounds wonderful, Willie,' and added, with a twinkle in her eye, 'Just the place for us.'

2

The girl at the check-in desk in Prestwick had assured them that their luggage would be transferred automatically to the New York-Phoenix plane, but Willie was not convinced and at New York in both the international and national terminals made a nuisance of himself to various officials, while Maggie kept telling him not to worry, the airline people knew their business. But he kept remembering having read of a passenger whose destination was Tokyo but whose luggage was sent to New York in both the weaken her faith, especially as he was beginning to draw confidence from it.

She turned out to be right. When they arrived at Phoenix some three hours later there were their suitcases on the carousel. It was damned near a miracle, thought Willie, but Maggie blithely took it for granted.

It was then eleven o'clock, dark but mild. The lights of a foreign city shone all round them. They were thousands of miles from home and very tired. Maggie remarked she was ready to drop but she said it with a brave smile.

It wasn't a time to expend further effort in finding a cheap hotel.

The taxi-driver watched nonchalantly as the old guy in the cloth cap struggled with the two cases, until the old guy asked to be taken to *The Excelsior*. Immediately the man's manner changed. He seized the cases and stowed them in his boot. He didn't call Willie 'sir' but then did American taxi-drivers ever call anyone 'sir'?

The taxi-driver was amused. He would enjoy telling his wife. Two old characters, Britishers, talking funny, and looking as if they'd to count every penny, and then saying, calm as you like, '*The Excelsior*' where the rates were four hundred dollars a day for a double. You just couldn't tell with foreigners.

'But, Willie,' whispered Maggie, with a giggle, 'isn't that the hotel where the girl on the plane said film stars stayed and rich people?'

'That's right, hen. We're rich, aren't we? For a few days anyway.'

She was looking out at the large white houses of Phoenix. 'It looks a nice town, Willie. Warm too.'

'I think where Elspeth is is a bit further north. It'll be colder there.'

'Well, we've brought warm clothes.'

Which meant that they were already sweltering, in Willie's case partly from nervousness, as the taxi drew up in front of the magnificent hotel.

A servant in a red jacket and white trousers ran down the steps to take their suitcases. He showed no surprise at Willie's cap or Maggie's hat, and did not return the taxi-driver's wink; indeed he frowned at its impertinence.

It so happened he was a member of the Teamsters' Union. That union had millions of dollars invested in the hotel. It was accustomed therefore to presidents, vice-presidents, and business agents being entertained free, as a reward for meritorious service. Nobody ever mistook them for film stars or genuine millionaires but they were given the same five-star treatment. This little guy with the funny way of talking could be from some far-off State like North Dakota where he was a big shot.

Meanwhile Willie and Maggie were being overawed by the size and splendour of the hotel. There was the great golden bird rising out of flames in the foyer, which was as vast as a cathedral; it had pillars too. There were real trees. The floor was covered by the biggest carpet they had ever seen. This was what impressed Maggie most, for she had once worked in the local carpet factory at home and knew quality when she saw it. 'That carpet, Willie,' she whispered, 'would have kept us busy for a month.'

At that time of night only one clerk was on duty at the reception desk. He was dressed like an undertaker, except that he had a red rose in his button-hole. He too was accustomed to uncouth unionists impersonating millionaires. In his experience many millionaires were uncouth too, so it was sometimes difficult to tell which was which. This little old guy for instance could be a business agent or the owner of a steelworks in Pittsburgh. What was unusual about him, though, was that he had brought his old lady with him and not a dolly-bird with voluptuous tits. More astonishing still, he was being more attentive to her than most tycoons were to their five hundred dollars a night bedmates.

So the clerk smiled and said 'Certainly, sir,' when Willie asked for a room for the night.

Americans, thought Willie, remembering the taxi-driver and the porter, were cool, affable people. They were such a mixed bunch themselves that a person would have to be a real oddity to faze them.

'From Glasgow, sir?' asked the clerk. 'Is that Glasgow, Scotland?'

'It is.' Willie knew there were several Glasgows in America. 'We're going on tomorrow to a place ca'd Holbrook. How do we get there?'

'By plane or bus or you could hire a car.'

'I think we'll fly. Have you any idea when the planes leave?'

The clerk consulted a time-table. 'There are three planes per day, at 9.30 a.m., 12.30 p.m., and 4.30 pm.'

'Could you book us two seats on the 12.30 please?'

'Certainly, sir.'

'Thanks.'

What magic there was in money, thought Willie. Wait till he got home and told them in the *Airlie Arms*. That was to say if they were still speaking to him.

The porter, waiting nearby, took their cases and led them to the lift. Even the lift was luxuriously carpeted; as was the corridor to their room, and the room itself. The whole hotel, Maggie said, would have kept her factory in work for a year.

The porter and the ex-porter looked at each other as the one offered the other a tip. They understood one another. The tip was taken. Thanks were given with a grin and accepted with a similar grin. They were the workers of the world who would, thought Willie, unite one day; perhaps in another thousand years.

Maggie was in raptures at the size and opulence of their room. The bathroom fascinated her. 'Fit for a queen,' she murmured.

She was remembering the queen whose picture hung on the living-room wall at home: Mary, Queen of Scots. On a visit to Edinburgh once Maggie had seen where Mary had slept in Holyrood Palace, and where she had relieved herself. She had been shocked. Even people living in slums nowadays had more civilised amenities. 'Fit for a queen,' she repeated, sadly.

In the bedroom, as she took out her nightclothes she said, 'Can we afford it, Willie?'

It was a financial, not a moral qualm.

'Aye, we can afford it, hen. Don't worry.'

'I'm not worrying. I'm just imagining that councillor's face if he could see us here.'

Yes, but most Glasgow people would see the joke: the ex-hospital porter and the ex-carpet factory-hand, spending the night in this hotel for the rich and famous.

Later, in bed, with her curlers in, Maggie said, 'Just imagine, Willie. We'll see Elspeth tomorrow.'

He hoped Elspeth would be fit to be seen. In his days at the hospital he had been horrified by the faces of cancer victims.

'This mission, Willie, will it be the same as the one in that postcard?'

'I don't know, hen. That one was in California.'

'What difference does that make?'

'Just that Elspeth's might no' be so grand.'

'I've been thinking that myself.'

3

Next day the porter was again helpful. He carried their cases down to the entrance and then found them a taxi. He directed it to the airport. Their seats to Holbrook had been reserved by telephone.

He astonished Willie by producing an autograph book and asking them to sign it. It was his daughter's, he said. She got him to obtain the autographs of all the famous people who stayed at the hotel. Among those had been Bette Davis and Clint Eastwood.

'We're not famous,' said Willie. 'Naebody's heard of us.'

'I told her about you, friend, and she wants your autograph; yours too, Mrs Hogg.'

Maggie was thrilled and signed with a flourish.

Willie's feeling of fraudulence vanished when he wrote Glasgow after his signature. He might not be famous but his native city was.

The 12.30 plane for Holbrook was small, with propellers. Willie explained it might be bumpier than the big planes they had been on yesterday, as it couldn't go so high above the clouds. What clouds? Maggie asked, and sure enough the sky was cloudless and blue.

Two black men occupied the seat in front of them. Maggie assured Willie in a whisper that she didn't mind, they looked very nice and were well-dressed. In any case she would have to get used to dark skins before she met the Indians on Elspeth's reservation. He smiled and patted her hand, but his heart sank a little. Up to now she had been wonderful. It would be a great pity if all her old fears and prejudices came rushing back.

The flight took less than two hours. Most of the time below was desert. Then ahead, as they came down to land, were mountains. The Grand Canyon was up there somewhere, said Willie.

'Will we see Elspeth right away, Willie?'

'I don't think we should try, hen. Better to put up at a hotel for the night and make arrangements to go oot to the mission the morrow. We'll be mair rested then.'

'But will we let them know we're coming?'

'Sure we will. We'll telephone from the hotel.'

'All right. Willie, there's something I'd like to say to you.'

'Say it then.'

'I hope you're not offended.'

'Of coorse I'll no' be offended. Whit is it, hen?'

'That's it, Willie. I don't think you should call me hen. Not here in America. They'll not understand. They'll laugh.'

He smiled. 'If that's whit you want, lass.' But didn't grown-ups here call each other 'baby'. They'd have a damned cheek laughing at 'hen'. Still, she was right. They were among foreigners. Elspeth herself was a foreigner now.

'Ask,' Willie's mother had told him when he was a child, 'and you'll find maist folk glad to help.' So at the airport at Holbrook he asked a taxi-driver to take them to a good but not too expensive hotel. 'Get in,' said the man, grumpily, but he drove them to a motel which they liked immediately. It consisted of little white cabins among trees and was situated in the heart of the town, handy for people without a car.

It was cooler up here, close to the mountains, but it wasn't coolness that was causing Maggie to shiver; it was the knowledge that after more than thirty years of separation she would soon see her sister again.

On the other side of the street was a motel whose units were in the shape of wigwams. Wait till I tell them in the *Arms*, thought Willie. 'Are you folks from Scatland?' asked the driver, as he was being paid.

'We are,' said Willie.

'My kid's a great collector of monsters. That one in Loch Ness, does it really exist?'

'Well, we live some distance from Loch Ness but there's a monastery on the banks at Fort Augustus. The monks there have said they've seen it. You wouldnae thinks monks would lie, would you?'

'I guess not.' Did the taxi-driver understand Willie was being ironical? Perhaps he had a prejudice against Catholics. There were men in Glasgow who wouldn't believe monks if they told them they'd seen a yellow bus.

Leaving their suitcases outside, they went into the manager's office. A notice on the door gave his name as Dave Rigby. Willie had half expected him to be wearing a headdress of feathers but he was wearing the next best thing, a big cowboy hat with silver stars all round it. He was a small man with a pleasant slow drawl and a grey moustache. Sure he had a vacant cabin. At that time of year he had a dozen. So they were from Scatland. He had a son in the navy stationed in Scotland, at a place called Holy Loch. Did they know it?

'Aye, we know it. It's not far frae Glesca where we come from.'

'Glesca?'

'Glasgow.'

'Now isn't that something. Marty often mentions Glasgow in his letters. He says the Scotch are the friendliest people he has ever met.'

So they must be if they were hospitable to Marty and his mates, considering how deeply they hated those abominable submarines and bombs.

'Well, Mr and Mrs Hogg of Glasgow, Scatland, welcome to Holbrook, Arizona. May I ask what has brought you to this neck of the woods?'

It was Maggie who answered. 'We've come to visit my sister. She's in charge of a mission near here, on an Indian reservation. Her husband wrote and told us she was ill.'

Willie wasn't watching the man's face very closely. That was another thing his mother had taught him. 'Dinnae stare at folk. It's rude.' But he couldn't help noticing the surprise followed by what looked like concern. Had Elspeth died?

'I've never met the lady,' said the manager, carefully. 'But I did hear she wasn't well. To tell the truth, we don't have much to do with the mission or the reservation either. Randy Hansen comes into town now and then for supplies, but Randy's no gossip.'

Was there something not quite right about the mission? Or was it that many Americans were ashamed of the way their governments had in the past killed many Indians and cheated the rest out of their land? It seemed the people of Holbrook didn't want them as neighbours.

The manager's affability was now tinged with uneasiness. He looked relieved when, having installed them in their cabin, he hurried back to his office, as if eager to get in touch with someone. Who, though? The local sheriff? 'There are strangers in town, sheriff. Look as if they've come to stir up trouble among the Redskins.'

I've seen too many Wild West films, thought Willie.

'It seems funny, Willie, him not having met Elspeth. She's been here five years.'

'Maybe her duties have kept her too busy to come into town much. He knows her man, anyway.'

The manager had said there was a good coffee shop in the main street, a short way off. They decided they would have a wash and then go for a stroll and a snack.

They were about to leave when the telephone in their cabin rang.

'It can't be for us,' said Maggie. 'Nobody knows we're here.'

It was the manager. 'Mr Hogg, I've got Randy Hansen on the line. He'd like to have a few words with you. Will I put him through?'

'Yes, please.'

As he waited Willie whispered to Maggie. 'It's her man, Hansen. He wants to talk to us.'

A voice spoke that Willie instantly trusted. It wasn't that it sounded friendly and sincere, though it did, it was also because he found in it, quietly expressed, a damn-the-lot-of-you humour, which Willie himself had often felt but had been too timid to show. But then any man who'd married Elspeth McCrae would have needed to show it or be crushed. And of course if your wife was dying of cancer, you had either to be defiant or sit and weep.

'Randy Hansen here, Mr Hogg. First, let me welcome you and Mrs Hogg to Arizona.'

'Thanks, Mr Hansen. Did you get my wire?'

'Yes, I did. May I say it was very courageous of you both to come, though I have also to say that it was a mistake.'

'A mistake? How could it be a mistake?'

'My advice is that you should return home immediately.'

'I'm afraid we cannae do that, Mr Hansen. We've come to see Elspeth and we're not leaving until we've seen her. How is she?'

There was a pause. 'I doubt if she'll last another week.'

Maggie, her head close to Willie's head. 'How does he know that. He's not a doctor.'

Hansen heard her. 'Doctors have come, Mrs Hogg, and have been sent away.'

'So she's getting no treatment?' said Willie.

'Unless you call prayers treatment.'

Willie didn't. 'Is she suffering?'

'She is.'

Willie remembered Dr Saunders muttering that he hoped she took pain-killers. Evidently she didn't.

Willie looked at Maggie's stricken face. 'Maybe he's exaggerating,' he said.

'No, Mr Hogg, I am not exaggerating. The position here is altogether desperate.'

Was there a tremor in his voice? Was he on the verge of tears, despite his defiance?

'But surely she's getting help,' said Willie. 'What about the people who employ her?'

'She won't listen to them. They want to close the mission. She refuses to let them. They want her to return to San Diego. She refuses to leave.'

So the trouble really was Elspeth herself. Willie didn't know whether to admire her faith or to call her mad.

'Where is she noo?' he asked. 'Is she no' able to talk to us herself?'

Another pause. 'She's not here. She is off on her rounds.'

'What do you mean?'

'Every day she visits a number of her parishioners. It's a large parish, fifty miles in any direction. So she's away for hours.'

'How is she able, if she's so ill?'

'Faith, Mr Hogg.'

'She doesn't walk, does she?' Or go on horseback.

'She drives an old jeep.'

'Does anybody go with her?'

'No. There's nobody.'

Maggie said, 'Why don't you go with her, Mr Hansen? You're her husband.'

'I'm disqualified, Mrs Hogg. You see, I'm not a believer.'

'How did she come to marry you, if you're not a believer?'

'That was fifteen years ago, Mrs Hogg. May I speak to your husband again.'

Maggie handed the telephone back to Willie. Tears were running down her cheeks.

'I can see, Mr Hogg, that I was being stupid and unreasonable asking you not to come out here. Of course you must. But be prepared for disappointment and grief. I shall call for you tomorrow morning at ten o'clock, if that's suitable.'

'We'll be waiting.'

'Very well. Till then, goodbye.'

'Goodbye.'

'He's coming for us the morrow at ten.'

Maggie went into the bathroom to wipe her face.

He sat and stared at the silent telephone. He shivered. There was something very wrong at the mission. Well, they would find out tomorrow what it was. He feared for Maggie.

He went over and called through the door. 'Are you a' right?'

The door opened and she came out, smiling. She had washed the tears off her face. She had put on fresh lipstick. She looked resolute.

He himself was still trembling.

'I thought we were going out for something to eat,' she said.

'So we were. So we will. Gie me a couple of minutes.'

In the bathroom he stared at himself in the mirror. Could he trust that fellow with the scared eyes? Could he depend on him in a crisis, and here was a crisis if ever there was one.

He would have to rely on Maggie. Two days ago that would have seemed ludicrous. Now it didn't.

She did then what she hadn't done for many years. She kissed him.

'Dear Willie,' she said.

She was not only brave, she was beautiful.

He knew then that he loved her.

It was curious, thought Willie, as they strolled down the main street, how Americans who had believed the Indians were savages now presented them as romantic, noble, and artistic. In the many souvenir shops there were large quantities of Indian artefacts, such as beaded buckskin costumes, bangles and necklaces of blue stones, moccasins, peace-pipes, headdresses of synthetic feathers, tomahawks, and even scalps with hair attached. He looked among the many postcards for one showing the Red Bluffs Apostolic Mission but saw none.

'Do you think I should take a scalp hame for Charlie McCann?' he asked, and added, to himself, 'He'll wish it was mine.'

As they went into the coffee shop he risked making a joke: 'I bet they have roast buffalo on the menu.'

'As long as it isn't roast squaw.'

It was the first time she had ever answered irony with irony.

In the coffee shop the placemats were in the shape of Indian heads but it was quiet and warm and they had a cosy corner to themselves. The young waitress was smiling and attentive, though she was dressed like an Indian maiden.

They had scrambled eggs with bacon and coffee. They would have preferred tea but only the cold lemon type was available.

'It's licensed,' said Willie. 'Would you mind if I have a glass o' wine?'

'I'll have one with you.'

'Good. It'll help us to relax.'

So far they hadn't spoken about their visit to the mission tomorrow. He did not know what Maggie was thinking and respected her too much to ask.

Back in the motel they lay down on their beds 'for a siesta' Maggie said.

She slept but he could not.

Would it have made a great difference to her life if she had had children? Would her blossoming have taken place many years ago and not waited till now, when she was nearly seventy? There could be no doubt that he had helped to delay it. Everybody, including himself, had thought it was she who had put a blight on him, but he realised now that it would be just as true to say that he had blighted her. He had taken away her self-confidence. He had never been fair to her.

These children, that had never been conceived, would have been middle-aged now, with children of their own. Maggie and he would have been at the centre of a small tribe. She would not have looked lonely then; because really she was the loneliest person he had ever known; lonelier even than himself. Surely it had been his fault. Lately she had felt that she had had her sister restored to her and she had been happy. Now it looked as if Elspeth would die soon. He would have to make up for that loss, during the few years that they had left.

How many young women would have agreed to be married by declaration in a lawyer's dusty office, with no white dress or flowers or wedding cake or sacred vows? She had done it to please him. But what was it she had done? What beliefs and principles of her own had she sacrificed? What longings? At that age, twenty-one, she must have had her own views of marriage and religion. They were hardly likely to be the same as his, and yet she had set them aside for his sake. God help him, he had always put it down to a consequence of her vagueness and confusion of mind, but now he realised, for the first time in over forty years, that it could have been on her part a conscious act of love and faith.

She slept for over four hours. It was dark in the room when she awoke. He had got up and was sitting in a chair.

'Why are you sitting in the dark, Willie?'

'I've been thinking.'

She laughed. 'You're always thinking. You were thinking the day I met you.'

'And where has it got me?'

'I'll tell you what it got you.'

'What?'

'A wife that's proud of you.'

'Maggie, you'll have me blushing.'

'If you had got the chance you could have become a doctor instead of a hospital porter, and you'd have made a good one.'

At least he would have been good at cheering up his patients while nature cured them.

'I never had the brains.'

Elspeth would have agreed to that.

She got up. 'You should have wakened me, Willie. You know I can't sleep at night if I've slept during the day.'

'It's still early. Just the back o' seven. We could go for a look at the toon wi' its lights, and have something to eat.'

'Do you know, Willie, that's something I've always liked, walking about a strange town at night.'

But, Maggie, how often have you done that? How many strange towns have you been in, day or night? Did all these towns exist in your imagination? And who was with you as you walked about your imaginary towns at night?

'It'll not be dangerous, will it? You read about so many murders in America.'

'We'll be safe enough if we keep to the main street.'

'I'll tell you something else, Willie, in the dark, so that you'll not see me blushing.'

'And what's that, pet?'

'I don't care for separate beds.'

So was he the one who had shrunk from intimacy? He remembered occasions when some display of passionate love on television had embarrassed him but not her.

'Well, we could push them together.'

'It's not quite the same.'

She went towards the bathroom. At the door she turned. 'If it wasn't for you, Willie, I'd have nobody.'

He was about to blurt out that she had her sister but stopped in time. Evidently she had prepared herself for Elspeth's death.

Why had he not said at once that if it wasn't for her he'd have nobody? All their married lives he had stopped short of any admission of absolute commitment. He had told himself that he was simply being truthful to his nature but had always suspected, as he did now, that he was being thrawn and mean-spirited. There was something in him which prevented him from handing himself over, body and soul, to another person. It had been the same when he was a child. 'Willie's no' like ither weans. When they rush forward he hings back.' And there had been the teacher with the rough frock and the cameo brooch at her throat. 'Willie Hogg's never going to let anyone be his sweetheart, is he?'

As they strolled along the main street of the strange town under the lights Maggie's arm kept squeezing his. She was letting him know that whatever happened she would not blame him and they would still have each other. She had come to this foreign country and found self-confidence and self-respect. What he had found he did not yet know.

They went into the coffee-shop for a light meal. They ordered cheeseburgers, coffee, and glasses of wine. There were other customers

who paid them little heed. He kept fearing that she would bring up
the subject of Elspeth but instead she spoke, with animation, of the
holiday in Rothesay many years ago when he had lost the oar.

'Remember the roses, Willie?'

There had been thousands of them in the little garden, red, white,
and yellow. The air had been sweet with their fragrance. Bees had
hummed and butterflies had fluttered. From the garden they had
looked down at the pier and watched the steamers come and go with
their funnels of different colours. What was the year? 1939. He was
twenty-five, she twenty-three. They had been married for two years,
It was so long ago, so many things had happened since, including a
war in which millions of people had been killed, but had there really
been an incident among the roses, one evening when Rothesay Bay
was red with sunset and the midges were out in brigades? Had he and
Maggie made love then, for the first and only time in the open air? (or
rather had attempted to, for the midges had made them give up). He
remembered Maggie's laughter. 'If we have a wee girl, Willie, we'll ca'
her Rosie.'

Yes, he remembered the roses.

'And the robins, Willie.'

'And the swans,' he said.

'And the big bird we saw flying over Canada Hill. We thought it
was an eagle.'

'It was an eagle.'

'And the sheep, Willie. Do you remember I was afraid of them. I
don't think I had ever seen sheep before.'

'I remember, lass.'

'Mrs McMaster.'

He didn't understand.

'That was the name of our landlady.'

How had she remembered that after so many years?

'I wonder if her cottage and garden are still there.'

'Likely the whole area's been turned into a car park.'

Usually while undressing for bed she turned her back on him and
while he was undressing kept her eyes closed, but that night she
stripped naked in front of him and was in no hurry to put on her
nightgown. Her breasts could have been those of a girl of twenty.

He was in his usual haste to get into his pyjama trousers, but she stopped him by putting her hand on his shoulder. She saw then what both of them had always united to prevent her from seeing. It was hardly fit to be seen. He remembered those baboons.

'Come into my bed, Willie,' she whispered.

Though he was trembling he could have sworn he smelled roses.

Next morning, as they waited in the sunshine with their suitcases ready, every time Maggie smiled at him, and she did it often, Willie felt famous. Deliberately he used Charlie McCann's sarcastic word. It wasn't the kind of fame that would have millions of people applauding him. He had no special talent. He could not cure Elspeth's cancer or lessen her pain or delay her death, but he could help to sustain Maggie in the difficult time ahead. If he could do that he would feel prouder of himself than any film star or political leader.

The manager had told them the mission was about twenty miles away. 'Dirt track most of the way. Randy could be late. That old truck he uses is always breaking down.'

Why then wasn't he supplied with a new one? Willie was sure now that one of the things wrong with the mission was lack of money.

Almost an hour late a beat-up, rusty, and very dusty pick-up truck rattled into the courtyard. Driving it was a man hardly any bigger than Willie himself, though he wore a cowboy hat high in the crown. His jacket, with holes in the elbows, was fit for a hired hand, not the boss's husband. He had a small neat white beard with moustache to match, like Buffalo Bill.

As he got down he glanced at their suitcases and shook his head.

'Sorry I'm late,' he said. 'Had to pick up some supplies and the damned thing wouldn't start. Well, I'm Randy Hansen.' He held out his hand. It was, Willie noticed, much too refined a hand for a man accustomed to hard manual work. He smiled. 'I used to be a watchmaker, Mr Hogg.' He turned to Maggie and shook hands with her too. She was fascinated, not by him or his beard or his hat but by his being Elspeth's husband and therefore her own brother-in-law.

'I hope I haven't kept you waiting too long,' he said.

'That's a' right,' said Willie. 'I was telling Maggie that time doesn't matter to country people the way it does to city people.'

'Courtesy matters everywhere, my friend.'

'So it does.' Willie felt relieved. He and Randy were going to get on all right. He wasn't sure about Maggie, though. She was still staring at him as if she thought him an imposter. Elspeth's husband would never have been so small or had a beard or holes in his jacket.

'These your suitcases?' he asked.

Willie nodded.

'Excuse me saying this, but I think you should leave them here. I'll bring you back later today.'

'Why should we do that?' asked Maggie. 'I want to be beside my sister.'

He hesitated 'Yes, I can see that.'

'We've come a long way, Mr Hansen,' said Willie.

'Yes, I know that. It's just that, well, you wouldn't find things comfortable.'

'I'm not looking for comfort,' said Maggie. 'I'll sleep on the ground if it's necessary. How is my sister this morning?'

'Just the same, only a little worse.'

'How can that be?'

But Willie understood. The disease got worse. The victim's faith remained strong

'Where is she?' asked Maggie. 'What's she doing at this very moment?'

'Helping a midwife. Praying for someone dying.'

'Is she out on her rounds again?' asked Willie.

'She is. Every day. Except Sundays.'

'Should she be doing that,' said Maggie, 'with her so ill?'

'No, she should not.'

'Why doesn't somebody else do it?'

'There's nobody else.' He took off his hat and stared into it. 'She sent you a message.'

They waited.

'What is it?' asked Maggie.

'She said she didn't want to see you. She said you should go home.'

'I don't believe it,' said Maggie.

But Willie did, and thought he understood. If it had been him dying of cancer, and ghastly with it, he might not have wanted to be seen; especially if he believed in God and was afraid He had forsaken him.

'We've come thoosands of miles,' he said. 'We just cannae turn and go back withoot seeing her, even if it's only for half an hour.'

Whose half-hour would that be? Theirs? Elspeth's? God's?

Though the sunshine was now warm he shivered.

'If you don't mind, Mr Hansen,' he said, 'please take us to the mission and let us see for oorselves whit the position is.'

'Very well.'

With Willie's help Hansen lifted the suitcases into the truck, among the cartons and sacks.

Maggie shouldn't forget, thought Willie, that this man was Elspeth's husband, closer to her therefore than any sister. If she was in pain so was he. If she died his grief would be the sorest and longest.

Hansen helped them into the cabin of his truck, where the seats were burst and the floor littered.

'Excuse me a minute,' he said, 'while I have a word with Dave Rigby.'

He went off to the manager's office.

'Do you trust that man, Willie?' asked Maggie.

'Aye, I do. Don't you?'

'I'm not sure. I don't think he's helping Elspeth as much as he could.'

He could have said that Elspeth might be difficult to help, with her stubbornness and her belief that God at the last minute would save her. But he said nothing.

Soon Hansen came out, and in a few minutes – the truck was reluctant to start – they drove off, with many rattles and bumps. Willie sat in the middle.

'Could you be more careful, please?' said Maggie. 'I've got a present for Elspeth in my case.'

It was a china plate with scenes of Glasgow depicted on it.

Soon they left the smooth public road and were lurching along a dirt track not much better than a dried-up river bed. Clouds of dust rose up. The windows had to be kept closed. They were thrown about the cabin. They passed a sign saying this was a Navajo reservation. Ahead, and all round, as far as Willie could see, was barren wilderness. Where were the green fields, the cattle, the sheep, the trees giving shade? Everything glared in the sunshine.

A thought occurred to Willie. 'Medicine men,' he shouted. 'Do Indians still have them?'

But would Elspeth, Christian missionary, look to heathens for alleviation or cure? Surely anyone with cancer would accept help from the Devil.

'Indeed they do. They're the wise men of the nations, but they're mostly very old and the young ones don't listen to them. Indians believe, in their moments of lucidity, that sound health of body and mind can only be achieved by a harmonious relationship with nature.'

Willie did not miss the bit about the moments of lucidity. 'I believe that too,' he said.

Hansen smiled. 'May I call you Willie?'

'If I can call you Randy.' Willie grinned. There would have been a few rude jokes about that name in the *Airlie Arms*.

'It's certainly a beautiful philosophy,' said Randy, 'if it could only be achieved; which isn't easy.'

'Impossible, I would say; in a place like this. Have the Indians got a council or something that runs the reservation?'

'They have. They call it a chapter. The present headman is called Bartholomew Simpson.'

'You're kidding. That's a Scottish name. Well, the Simpson bit is.'

'His deputy's called Henry McKellar. That's Scottish too, I believe.'

'It certainly is. How did they get these names?'

'I suppose their grandfathers borrowed them from their white oppressors.'

'Who must have been Scottish?'

'I expect the Scots have done their share of oppressing in the past, Willie.'

Willie grinned. 'In the service of their English masters. I thought Indians had romantic names like Swift Arrow and Laughing Water.'

'So they have but they do not use them. The contrast between the dream and the reality is too painful.'

'I can believe that. This is just a wilderness, isn't it? I've never seen so much sky.'

'At night the stars are a wonder to behold.'

'This is desert, isn't it?'

'You could call it that, though it's not sand, but earth and stones.'

'Nothing seems to grow on it.'

'Cactus does. And sagebrush.'

'Sagebrush?' Willie remembered a favourite story of his boyhood, Riders of the Purple Sage.

'And Joshua trees.'

'Why Joshua?'

'That I could not say. In Spring there are innumerable wild flowers, so tiny you have to kneel to see them.'

Willie remembered Angus McPhie's rapturous accounts of the machairs on Barra. 'Your shoes get yellow with pollen.'

'But nothing edible?' he said.

'Nothing edible.'

'Because of the lack of water?'

'For that reason only.'

'Nae springs?'

'Not hereabouts.'

'Whit does the mission do for water?'

'It has to be hauled eight miles. One of my present chores.'

'How long have you been living here yourself, Randy?'

'Well, I suppose as long as Elspeth – five years. But I don't live here all the year round. My home's in San Diego. My stay this year has been extended.'

Willie didn't need to ask why.

Maggie was listening. 'This home in San Diego, is it Elspeth's too?'

'Yes.'

'Why doesn't she live in it then? I'm sure San Diego's a nicer place to live than here.'

'It's one of the nicest places in the world, Mrs Hogg. But she will tell you God sent her here.'

That silenced Maggie.

'How do the Indians keep themselves?' asked Willie. 'There's no work and nothing will grow.'

'Government handouts.'

'I see.'

Just then a truck could be seen coming towards them, at high speed. It passed them in a shower of dirt and stones. It looked new and was brightly painted. Three young Indians were in the cabin. They looked smartly dressed.

'Were they Navajos?' he asked.

'This is all Navajo land.'

'They looked prosperous enough.'

'They are prosperous.'

'How is that?'

'They were lucky. Water was found on the part allocated to them. So they have fields of corn, herds of cattle, and even an industry or two. Also a trading-post which they operate themselves so that the prices are reasonable, and not rip-offs.'

'But if they're so prosperous why don't they help the others that aren't?'

'In your native Glasgow, Willie, do the inhabitants of prosperous areas help those of impoverished areas?'

'Not so as you would notice it.'

'It is the same here. Navajos are simply members of the human race.'

'But members of the human race do help one another.'

'It has been known. Here in fact is an opportunity for us to demonstrate it.'

He stopped the truck beside some large red boulders. In their shade lay a man in a white shirt and blue jeans. A cowboy hat covered his face. His boots had high heels.

Willie had seen too many drunks to be in any doubt. Here was one Indian whose relationship with nature was not harmonious.

'He'll get roasted lying there,' he said.

'Is he drunk?' asked Maggie.

'I'm afraid he is, Mrs Hogg,' said Randy. 'Liquor is forbidden but they always manage to find some.'

'The old fire-water?' said Willie. 'How did he get here?'

'I expect he started out walking from town last night but didn't make it.'

'So he's spent the night there?'

'I would think so. You are looking at a relic of a once proud nation.'

'Do many of them get drunk?'

'As many as can afford it. Temporary oblivion.'

'I'm surprised Elspeth allows it,' said Maggie. 'She was always against drink.'

'She still is, Mrs Hogg. She preaches against it without avail. It has been one of her greatest difficulties.'

Willie was beginning to get some idea of those difficulties. Running a mission here was no job for a woman of sixty-two.

'Meanwhile,' said Randy, 'what do we do about Henry?'

'Henry? Do you know him? Or do you ca' them a' Henry?'

'I know him. Henry Begay. One of ours. Now do we take him home, involving ourselves in a long inconvenient detour, with risk of damage to the truck, not to say to ourselves, or do we just leave him lying there?'

'If we did would he be a' right?'

'With luck he might be. On the other hand he might find coyotes have bitten off his fingers.'

'We can't leave him there,' said Maggie, 'though he deserves it.'

'Thank you, Mrs Hogg. That's one vote in favour of succouring him. What do you say, Willie?'

In Glasgow Willie had left drunks lying in the gutter, but somehow it was different here. In this vast empty hostile land, under this immense callous sky, humanity must be as strong as steel, if it was not to crumble and blow away like this constant dust.

'I agree with Maggie. We've got to help him.'

'You are both credits to your native city.'

First Randy removed the hat. There was revealed a face Willie had seen dozens of times in Wild West films, usually daubed with war paint and wearing expressions of fierce haughtiness. Here it was simply stupefied.

They got him to his feet. There was a stink of cheap booze off him. His eyes were glazed and senseless. He said nothing.

With much effort they heaved him up into the truck, among the sacks, boxes, canisters of gas, and the two suitcases. Maggie watched anxiously through the small window.

Willie did his best to make him comfortable. He didn't want him to waken up with a crick in his neck as well as a blinding headache.

They drove on again.

'Expect no thanks,' said Randy.

'Considering whit oor kind hae done to his kind we'd have a damned cheek looking for thanks.'

'Willie, you disappoint me. I took you for a realistic man.'

'But you can't deny that the white man stole the Indians' land or the best part of it anyway.'

'It was worse than that, Willie. The Indians never claimed owner-ship of land. The idea would have seemed alien and repugnant to them. The Great Spirit gave the earth to all His creatures. So when the white man arrived he didn't only grab what didn't belong to him, he also outraged a noble and time-honoured tradition.'

'Why did you say then I disappointed you?'

'Because it would be better forgotten.'

'It would suit the white man to forget it.'

'It would suit the red man even more. His only hope of salvation, in my opinion, is to merge with the rest of the population and not allow himself to be hidden away in reservations like this. America is made up of English, Irish, Scots, Poles, Swedes, Germans, Mexicans, and many others. These have all united to make one nation. Why don't the Indians join us?'

'Well, why don't they?'

Randy looked across at Maggie. 'Are you all right, Mrs Hogg?'

'My insides are shaken to pieces but I'm all right.'

'I thought you looked pale.'

Willie was still waiting for Randy to tell him why the Indians didn't join the rest of Americans.

'I think, Willie, because they feel doomed in their hearts. Wounded Knee meant the end of the Indian nation, body and soul.'

'Can a whole nation feel doomed?' As he asked Willie knew another nation that if it didn't feel doomed it damned well ought to. He meant Scotland, the only country in history that, offered a meagre ration of home rule, declined it.

They had now left the track and were bumping over the desert itself, making for no where at all so far as Willie could see. In the far distance were hazy hills of strange shape.

Suddenly there was a hollow. At first he thought it a rubbish dump. Tin cans, bottles, plastic containers, the carcase of a bicycle, and a dead dog. Then he saw the house, a hogan Randy called it, a square hut built of logs cemented together with mud. Smoke came out of a hole in the roof. What fuel was being burned? Willie wondered. No coalman passed that way.

'It's like a tinkers' camp,' said Maggie.

'Is that where Henry lives?' asked Willie.

'It is.'

'Where's his nearest neighbour?'

'About two miles away, Henry's a great landowner.'

'Land that's worth nothing.'

'True. But worth a fortune if water was ever found. Geologists come regularly to look for it.'

'I bet if water was found here these Indians would be pushed off into another desert.'

'Very likely.'

They lifted the drunk man and laid him carefully on the ground. Willie gave him a pat on the shoulder.

A woman had appeared at the door of the hogan. She was fat and dirty. She wore a dress down to her ankles. Her hair was almost as long, in two thick black tresses. She might have been carved of mahogany, she stood so still. A child peeped from behind her.

'His mother?' whispered Willie.

'His wife.'

'But she looks twenty years older.'

'Indian women seem to age faster than the men. They also go to fat.'

'Can you talk to her in her own language?'

'No. Elspeth speaks it fluently.'

Now there was a marvel, a woman born and bred in the east end of Glasgow able to talk to Navajo Indians in their own language.

'Does she understand English?'

'Yes, but she'll pretend she doesn't.'

'You'd think we'd murdered him, the way she's looking at us.'

In a minute, Willie imagined, the arrows would start to fly. Was that the bugle of the Seventh Cavalry he heard? No, it was an insect buzzing in his ear.

They got back into the truck and drove off.

'Are all the women like her?' asked Maggie.

'Some are older and fatter.'

'And Elspeth looks after *them*?'

'They are her parishioners, Mrs Hogg.'

'Is she a kind of minister then?'

'She is.'

'Good gracious!'

'Are they Christians,' asked Willie, 'or is she still trying to convert them?'

'She thinks she has converted them but I doubt it. They use the church as a meeting-place and they sing hymns, for they like the tunes.

Cheery tunes sung lugubriously. God knows what they are really thinking. They must be the most uncommunicative people in the world. There are of course material benefits in belonging to the mission. Every now and then members of churches in San Diego send up large consignments of goods to be distributed. In fact one is expected next week.'

It would be the last, thought Willie, but he did not say it.

5

The bright desolation had at last begun to distress Maggie. 'Where is everything?' she asked. 'Where is everybody?'

Mile after mile there continued to be nothing but dry stony earth and hazy blue sky. They saw no other people or animals even, though Randy said there were some, such as lizards lurking among the rocks. Was this the kind of wilderness, Willie wondered, that Christ had spent some time in. Had it been to regain His faith? Or to escape from the pollutions of humanity? Or to talk to God? If I was out there alone for a day or two, thought Willie, I'd be talking to God myself, even though I don't believe He exists, and I'd be doing it through swollen lips.

Randy remarked that in two or three weeks snow would fall and lie till Spring. It was that which made the flowers grow. Wood for fuel had to be brought in at great expense. In summer the desert was so hot that if you picked up a stone it would burn your hand.

No wonder, thought Willie, the people who live here are uncommunicative. What had they to say except to declare their despair? And silence did that even better.

They were now heading for a high rugged cliff of red rock. As they got nearer Willie could make out a collection of shacks, made of wood with corrugated iron roofs. He thought at first it was a village, an attempt by some of the people to gather together and resist the terrifying loneliness. But no, it was the mission: a poorer place altogether than the one at Santa Barbara. A board carried the words Red Bluff Apostollic Mission, in faded white paint. But should Apostolic have two 'l's? The church, identified by a Cross (tilted to one side) was the largest building, but even so looked very small in that great space. Some fifty yards from it was what looked to be an occupied house; smoke rose from its rusty chimney. Was this the bishop's palace? There were other shacks, neglected and dilapidated. He was to learn afterwards that one contained a defunct generator; this was Randy's retreat. One structure was noticeable: a wooden box as high as a tall man and as wide as a fat one – outside lavatory, the cludgy, to use a Glasgow word never more appropriate than here. It stood by itself, a good hundred yards from any of the other buildings. One's trek to it would be conspicuous. God help anyone with diarrhoea.

But had Christ's sanitary facilities been any better, or Mary, Queen of Scots'? *They* didn't have the benefit of disinfectants.

They climbed down from the truck.

'Is this it?' asked Willie.

'This is it.'

'God's outpost?'

'That's right.'

Maggie was staring all about her. 'Where are the shops?' she asked.

'There's only one shop, Mrs Hogg,' said Randy. 'Miles away. A trading post where prices are twice as high as in town. The Indians have to cash their welfare cheques there.'

An old mangy dog was lying in the shade. It raised its head to look at the newcomers, decided there was nothing to be had from them, yawned, and went to sleep again.

'Where's the staff?' asked Willie. The situation was so bizarre he almost found it funny, especially as he compared it with the elegant white buildings and palm trees and flowers of Santa Barbara. 'Apart from you and Elspeth.'

'I am not a member of the staff, Willie. Like yourselves I am a visitor. I come here only occasionally, and then for two or three weeks. This has been my longest stay.'

'But who cooks the meals? Who sweeps out the church? Who washes the clothes?' And who emptied the can?

'I do, in the meantime. But not very well, I'm afraid. You see, Willie, this place is finished. Those who finance it would close it down tomorrow if it wasn't for Elspeth.'

'But surely they know she's not well.'

'Yes, they know. They've been to see her, to plead with her, they've sent doctors, but when she tells them it is God's will that she remains here, being religious fanatics themselves, they can't contradict her and tell her she's talking nonsense.'

'So they've decided to wait till – well, till God gives her permission to leave; that's to say when she dies.'

'That is how they would put it themselves. They don't expect to have to wait long.'

'Then what will happen to this place?'

'I expect the buildings will be used as firewood. Perhaps that would be the most useful purpose they ever served.'

Willie could tell what that uncharacteristic burst of bitterness hinted at. Randy and Elspeth must have loved each other when they got married fifteen years ago. It could be that they still did. What could a man do when his wife discovered that she loved God more than she did him? And what could a woman do whose husband was jealous of a God he did not believe in?

Maggie had been going about, inspecting. She came back, on the verge of hysteria, Willie thought.

'Where is she, Willie? Where is my sister?'

'She'll not be long, pet.'

'Can't we go and look for her?'

'I wouldn't advise it,' said Randy. 'She could be anywhere out there.'

'Do you care, Mr Hansen, do you care where she is?'

'Yes, Mrs Hogg, I care.'

She believed him. 'I'm sorry, Mr Hansen. I'm upset. I don't know what I'm saying. This isn't what we expected, is it, Willie?'

'It certainly isn't.'

Yet Willie himself was fascinated. He had always had a hankering for lonely places and here was loneliness indeed and in spite of his Socialist Sunday school upbringing he had had all his life a sense of wonder, a feeling that, if conditions were right, which might happen once in a life-time, unaccountable things could happen. Was this such a place? Were these the right conditions?

Meanwhile a familiar, easily accountable thing was happening to him: he needed to go a place. He eyed it with dismay. He wondered if it was permissible to squat behind one of the buildings – not the church – but if every one did that the place would be littered with turds. He decided to try and wait.

'I'd like to see inside the house,' said Maggie. 'Is there someone there? There seems to be a fire.'

'A stove. I ought to prepare you, Mrs Hogg, or rather warn you. You may find it untidy or worse.'

'What can you expect if there's nobody to clean it?'

'Why can't some of the Indian women be employed?' asked Willie.

'It has been tried. They did not prove satisfactory.'

'I'll tackle it myself,' said Maggie. 'Will you help me, Willie?'

'I will that.'

As a matter of fact he was a more proficient and energetic housewife than she. She would go into daydreams with brush or duster in hand. But here was a new Maggie.

'There are, though, assistants of a sort,' said Randy, pausing at the door. 'Three of them.'

'Three!' cried Willie. 'So why is everything dirty?'

'You will see. Don't be afraid, Mrs Hogg. They are harmless.'

Is he talking about cats or pet monkeys, Willie wondered.

The door opened straight into the living-room. Round a stove in the centre were crouched, on grubby armchairs, three old, very old, Indian women, with seamed faces the colour of tobacco. Two were smoking pipes, the other a cigar. All three wore long black dresses adorned with glittering beads. They had striped blankets over their shoulders. Their hair should have been snow white but was black as soot; it was bound with red ribbons. Round their shrivelled necks hung necklaces of blue stones.

They glanced up at the visitors and then went on with their silent contemplation. Were they remembering the days of their childhood long ago when the Navajos were a proud nation and lived amidst green fields, beside sparkling rivers? Or were they simply in a senile dwam? Willie could not smell booze; only woodsmoke, tobacco, and greasy dishes.

Who were they? Had they been cast out by their families and taken in by Elspeth? Did she, after her day's darg of travelling, healing, and praying, come home to take care of them? Elspeth the saint.

He was afraid for Maggie. These old women were creatures of nightmare, and Maggie in the past had often wakened out of sleep, whimpering and weeping. But when he turned to her he found her smiling at him. Don't look so alarmed, Willie, her smile said. This isn't the Cowcaddens, you know, though there were houses there where, if you went in unexpected, you'd see sights as strange as this.

Keep the heid, Hogg, he told himself. It could have been a lot worse. It could have been a hundred years ago and he and Maggie had been captured by Indians who were about to flay them alive, while these old women watched and cackled.

He was proud of this new Maggie or perhaps it was just the old Maggie that he had never made enough effort to discover. She was not going to give up just because of a kitchenful of dirty dishes, dust inches deep everywhere, a sour smell, a lack of hot water, and three old witches.

Randy showed them the two bedrooms. One was the old women's; it had no beds, only blankets on the floor. The other was Elspeth's. It had a bed, so narrow and hard-looking that it was like what a nun might lie on as a penance. But relief was coming, Randy said. The truck from San Diego would bring beds, among other household goods. The trouble was Elspeth probably wouldn't accept one more comfortable. Others' needs must come first.

Willie felt sad that this was where his sister-in-law lay at night, trying to sleep in spite of great pain. He also felt angry but did not know against whom or what. In hospital Elspeth would have been more comfortable, drugged with the most effective painkillers. Death would have come to her with some dignity. If it came to her here in this mean little room, who would know, who would benefit?

'You can see, Mrs Hogg,' said Randy, as they went back into the living-room, 'why I suggested you and Willie should return to Holbrook and spend the night in the motel. You can still do so.'

Why not? thought Willie. Where were he and Maggie to sleep? 'But I want to be near my sister, Mr Hansen,' said Maggie, 'and there's a lot of work for me to do. Can you get me some hot water, Willie?'

'Sure.'

With Randy's help Willie filled a pot with cold water and put it on the gas cooker. He was reminded of makeshift meals in another desert.

Maggie went to Elspeth's room to take off her hat and coat. When she came back she was wearing her tartan apron and had her sleeves rolled up, but first she whispered into Willie's ear. Would he escort her to the lavatory? Only for the first time. She'd go on her own afterwards. She'd used outside lavatories before.

So he stood outside watching her walk with that unconscious elegance towards the cludgy. He had tears in his eyes and yet he was wondering, amidst his love for her, whether there was any toilet paper. And when had the can last been emptied?

Soon she was walking back towards him as delicately as if from a bathroom as splendid as that in the *Excelsior* hotel.

Well done, Maggie.

'Is it bad?' he asked.

She crinkled her nose. 'Bad enough.'

'Is there any toilet paper?'

'Some old newspaper.'

He remembered his mother cutting newspaper into neat squares.

'My turn noo,' he said, trying to sound cheerful but not succeeding.

She patted his cheek. She knew how fastidious he was about such things. When they had lived in Allander Street, with the shared lavatory, he had often lamented other users' carelessness.

It could have been worse but not much. The wooden seat had been soaked and dried a thousand times. There were flies and bluebottles, dead and alive. There was a black spider that looked venomous. Had Maggie seen it? She hated spiders. There were chinks through which the clean and sanitary desert could be seen and envied. There was a stink. One advantage would be that no one would linger there. Not for the first time Willie thought that if he had been given the job of designing the human body he would have done better than this messy arrangement of bowels and bladder. It worked, he couldn't deny that, in his own case it was still working after seventy years, but it was crude.

As soon as it was dark he would empty the can, scour it out, and put in fresh disinfectant. Tomorrow he and Randy would go into town and buy a few luxuries, to make life more bearable: toilet paper for one. The Fund would pay.

6

Glasgow would have been proud of them, especially of Maggie. She soon lost her distrust of the gas cooker and boiled several potfuls of water on it. Looking in drawers she found dishtowels, tablecloths, and napkins – wedding presents, Randy remarked. Once or twice he was on the point of giving up and sneaking off to his den but Maggie wouldn't allow him. The time to rest was when the work was done.

Afterwards, when the house was looking reasonably clean and

smelling a lot fresher, she helped Willie to make lunch for them all including the three old women: potatoes, canned soup, canned meat, canned beans, and canned peaches. She used dishes that also had been wedding presents. As far as Randy knew they had never been used before. She had everyone eating at a table covered with a white cloth. Willie would have preferred the old women to eat apart for it turned out that they lacked teeth, let alone table manners, and their hearty slurpings took away what little appetite he had.

Just the same he was pleased and moved when, after the meal, one of the old women, without a word, took a necklace from her own neck and put it round Maggie's. Maggie was at her bravest then. She stood still. She did not grue or shrink back. She smiled. She murmured thanks.

The other old women came forward and touched her on the shoulder.

Randy was impressed. 'They know you're Elspeth's sister, Mrs Hogg,' he said.

'Anybody can see the resemblance, Mr Hansen.'

Willie never could.

'But it's not that. They're honouring you for your own sake.'

'Me? I'm just an ordinary Glasgow housewife.'

'And therefore the salt of the earth,' said Willie.

'Don't be daft, Willie.' But she was very pleased.

She was also very tired. Willie urged her to lie down and rest, but where was a suitable place? Elspeth's bed? But Elspeth would need it if she came back exhausted. In the church, said Randy, there was a small room which Elspeth kept as her own private refuge. It had a camp bed and an easy chair. She rested there before and after services. She did not let anyone else use it but surely she would make an exception in the case of her sister, especially as Mrs Hogg had worked so hard.

Maggie and Willie went across to the church to inspect the room. The church itself reminded Willie of his Socialist Sunday school long ago; very plain, with rows of uncushioned wooden forms.

In the anteroom the camp bed was low, with shaky legs, but it would do, Maggie said. There was a black robe hanging from a hook on the back of the door. 'You'll not go away if I fall asleep?'

'No, lass.' And when he had made her comfortable, with a

blanket spread over her, he went back into the church to have a closer look.

An ordinary kitchen table, covered with a red and black cloth, was the altar. On a lectern that looked home-made was a large Bible, in a strange language; as were the hymn books piled on a chair. He supposed it was Navajo. He marvelled again that Elspeth could read it.

There was an old piano. He sat down at it. He had never had a lesson in his life but as a boy he had had a good ear and had been able to play simple tunes. He had been let into his grandmother's parlour to entertain himself and his friends at her piano. The privilege had been taken away when she had heard him playing the naughty song: 'Auntie Mary had a canary, Up the leg of her drawers.'

He played a few notes and then stopped. Maggie was trying to get to sleep.

'Don't stop for me, Willie,' she called. 'Play "Sweet Afton" ' It had been her mother's favourite.

'I'll try.'

At first he made a mess of it. The piano didn't help. But he persevered and at last got it almost right.

'That was lovely, Willie.'

'Any other special request?'

'Could you manage "Loch Lomond"?'

Not only did he play it, he sang it too.

Would he and Maggie ever see those bonnie banks again?

'Should you be playing songs like that in a church?' called Maggie.

'I don't think God will mind.'

'Especially as he's a Scotsman. Do you remember old Mr McDiarmid? He was fond of saying God was a Scotsman.'

'When he had a few drams.'

Willie remembered Tam McDiarmid for another reason. He had been one of the worst lingerers in the lavatory in Allander Street.

'Play "Sweet Afton" again, Willie, and then I'll go to sleep.'

He played it *con amore*, as the Tallies said.

After a while he got up and went quietly to see how she was. She was asleep, not on the bank of the Ayrshire river but in the midst of this Arizona desert. He sat and watched her for a while. She had the necklace round her neck.

He thought about Elspeth. He really shouldn't be amazed at her ending up as a missionary among Red Indians. There had always been such a destiny waiting for Elspeth McCrae.

7

Maggie was still asleep when, while it was still daylight, the jeep came back.

Willie pulled aside a curtain and peeped out. His heart beat fast. What did a saint of sixty-two look like?

Thinking that no one saw her the white-haired woman did not try to hide her weariness as she climbed down. She stumbled and might have fallen if she had not held on to the vehicle. He had been remembering her as tall and strong, but she was stooped and thin. Her legs, which he had once likened to a football player's could hardly support her. He had the impression of utter exhaustion, as if she was carrying a burden much too heavy for her but which she resolutely refused to put down. Was it, though, a useless burden? He did not have the arrogance to say it was.

Randy appeared but not to greet her. There was no exchange of greeting.

Feeling guilty, Willie watched husband and wife meet. There was no contact. Randy did not show concern. She did not expect it. Willie felt angry. He had not thought Randy would be so unforgiving.

As if it was casual gossip, Randy was telling her about Willie and Maggie's arrival. She glanced towards the church. Just in time he let the curtain fall back into place.

If she made a scene about their trespassing in the church he would be patient and accept blame, but he would not let her abuse Maggie. He had had to reprove her for it many years ago but she hadn't been a saint then. He rebuked himself for the use of the word though he had not meant it sarcastically.

The door opened and she came in. She was wearing faded blue jeans and an open-necked sleeveless blouse, also blue. He would never have recognised her. What had happened to those proud breasts which the youths of the Cowcaddens used to whistle at? As well as white her hair was unkempt and dusty: he remembered it as black and neat. She held herself straight as she had always done but previously without effort.

Now he saw strain in all of her; her neck and mouth twitched with it. Her head kept wanting to drop forward, as dead people's heads did. He had seen too many not to know that. If she did let go, even for a minute, it would all collapse, this dignity, this defiance of pain, this carrying of the burden. She would then become pitiable and human. But she would not let go until given permission: that was when God saw fit to take her, or when she died as Willie himself would say.

What was it for, this endurance of extreme suffering? In the department store that was heaven would a few Indian souls be missed?

She stared at him and shook her head, smiling.

'Hello, Elspeth,' he said.

'What is an unbeliever like you doing in the Lord's house, William Hogg?'

Expecting hostility he thought she was being hostile but could it be that she was making fun of him?

'I don't think he minds, Elspeth. He hasn't said so anyway.'

'Still the same wee gallus Glasgow keelie?'

Did she remember what gallus and keelie meant? Or had she been away too long?

'Where is Margaret?' she asked.

'In there. Asleep.' Disturb not her dream, he thought, quoting the song.

She went over and opened the door quietly. She did not go in but stood gazing at her sister.

Willie remembered the ample backside she had had in her Glasgow days; now it was sadly shrunk. He noticed too her left hand clenching and unclenching. It was as if she wanted to make an appeal to someone, if she could find someone who would understand. Randy would not do. Nor Maggie. What about me, Elspeth? Who better than a wee gallus Glasgow keelie to see the joke?

She closed the door and came back to him. 'She doesn't look well, William.'

'She's tired. You look very tired yourself, Elspeth.'

'You should never have brought her here. The journey's been too much for her.'

'She wanted to come. She wanted to see you.'

'Yes.'

'And I would have thought you would have wanted to see her.'

'Does she still visit our mother's grave every Sunday?'

'Rain or shine.'

'Do you go with her?'

'Always. There are busy streets to cross.'

'Yes.' She smiled, remembering those streets. 'Sometimes I think I would like to see Glasgow again.'

'You might still manage it.'

But they both knew she never would.

'How could you afford to come here, William? It must have cost a great deal.'

Afterwards he would tell her about the Fund. If it pleased her to think of it as a miracle, well so it had been in a way. 'Neighbours helped. I'll tell you about it later.'

'Thank you for bringing her here, William.'

He felt embarrassed.

'God will reward you.'

It was like a blessing. His blood turned cold.

'And for looking after her so well.'

He could have wept. Criticism he had expected and could have borne, but not this praise. 'I could have done it a lot better. I've not been fair to her.'

'Neither was I fair to her. Nor to you.'

He had to change the subject. 'We've met Randolph.' He did not like to say Randy. 'He's been very obliging. He brought us from Holbrook.'

'He does well for one who refuses to understand.'

Now what did that mean? Randy was an intelligent man. It wasn't a case of his refusing to understand; he just couldn't. Every delicate little bit of the watches he had made had had its function which could be seen and explained. There were no mysteries. But, Randy, there were. The lizard I saw on the window ledge a minute or two ago, those stars beginning to appear in the sky. All my life I have reached out for something I never got hold of. You would say because it was never there. Yes, but I find myself still reaching out.

'Maybe he doesn't show it, Elspeth, but he's very concerned about you.'

'And I about him, William.'

Your body and his soul.

'He thinks you should be in hospital. So does Maggie. So do I.' But did he? Going into hospital might relieve her pain and delay her death a little, but it would prevent her fulfilling her purpose, whatever in Christ's name she thought that purpose was.

'They could do nothing for me in hospital.'

'They could make it easier for you. They could take away your pain.'

'And take away my joy.'

Joy? Had he heard right? Yes, she had said joy, and had tried to say it joyfully and was now trying to look joyful. Some kind of satisfaction might be found in ending her days doing what she believed God had called on her to do, but joy? Yet when he looked at her more closely, in the crimsoning church, what he saw on her pale strained face and in her eyes that were full of pain was joy. But was it the joy of a woman crazy with pain and disappointment?

She did not sound crazy. 'Well, William, there's work to be done. Supper to be prepared.'

He felt angry then, with Randy, skulking in his den and consoling himself with Mozart. The bugger should have been helping to prepare supper.

'No, Elspeth. You go and rest. Maggie and me will prepare supper.'

'I believe she made lunch.'

'And did it very well.'

'Good for her.'

'You go and rest. We'll be over as soon as she wakens. She asked me to waken her as soon as you got back.'

'No. Let her rest.'

'All right, but we'll be over shortly. Wait till we come.'

'Very well.'

When she was gone he went and sat beside Maggie. He closed his eyes and clasped his hands. He wasn't praying, though. He would have been mortified if his friends of the *Airlie Arms*, peeping in, had accused him of praying.

8

Maggie slept for another half-hour and awoke in the dark with anxious sighs until she was aware of him sitting there. She put out her hand to take his.

'I didn't know where I was for a minute,' she said.

No wonder, he thought. Where you are, hen, is as unlikely a place on the face of the earth for you and me to be.

'Are you feeling rested noo?' he asked.

'Yes. I feel fine. Has Elspeth come back yet?'

'She has.'

Maggie sat up. 'Why didn't you waken me, Willie? I asked you to.'

'We thought we should let you finish your sleep. You needed it.'

'Have you seen her then? How is she, Willie?'

'She looked in at you, Maggie.'

'You're not telling me how she is.'

Because I don't know what to say. Should I say, very ill but joyful? Or very ill and pretending to be joyful? Or very ill but also very brave, which we would have expected, but humorous too, which we wouldn't? She called me a wee gallus Glasgow keelie. He fell back on the typical Scottish answer: 'She's a' right.'

'How can she be all right if she's dying. Is she dying, Willie?'

She was asking an expert. He had seen hundreds of dying people. 'Aye, Maggie, but it's no' getting her doon. She seems happy enough.'

'Happy? How can anyone with cancer be happy?'

'Don't forget, Maggie, she thinks God's looking after her. You and me can't understand that, but she believes it.'

'No, I can't understand it. Did she remember me?'

'Of coorse. She asked if you still put flo'oers on your mither's grave every Sunday.'

'Imagine her remembering that!'

'She remembers lots of ither things too. She called me a wee gallus Glesca keelie.'

'Did she? Why, what were you saying?'

'She was joking.'

'Our Elspeth joking?'

'You'll find her greatly changed, Maggie.'

'What's she doing now?'

'Resting, I hope. I told her you and me would make the supper.'

'Good. So we will. But I've got to go to that awful place first.'

'Just nip behind the church. Naebody will see. It's dark.'

'Would she mind?'

'She'll never know.'

'All right.' She got up, with his assistance. Together they crept out of the church. There were lights from the house windows. Maggie disappeared round the gable of the church.

She soon came back. 'It reminds me of the time the Guildry went camping at Balloch.'

But you were a wee lassie of ten then, Maggie, not an old woman of sixty-seven.

'I want to be calm in my mind, Willie, when I meet her. I don't want her to be ashamed of me.'

'She knew you'd made lunch and cleaned the place up. Randy told her. She said you'd done very well.'

'Do you think she meant it, Willie?'

'She said it in the church. She'd have to speak the truth there, wouldn't she?'

'She always spoke the truth everywhere.'

Well, as she had seen it anyway. Maggie and he had often been the victims of her ruthless truth-telling.

They made for the house. It was turning chilly. Maggie shivered. 'It's a pity there's no bathroom. I'd like to give myself a good wash, Willie.'

'I'll bring you a basinful of hot water in Elspeth's room.'

'Thanks, Willie.'

Elspeth was not resting in her room; she was busy in the kitchen. Randy was setting the table, putting the knives where the forks should have been. The old Indian women seemed to have retired for the night.

Then came the meeting of the sisters. Elspeth came into the living-room. She faced Maggie across the table.

'Well, Margaret, this is a surprise.'

'So it is, Elspeth.'

'How are you?'

'I'm fine. How are you yourself?'

'Well enough.'

It was as if they had last met a week ago.

Willie had not expected an emotional meeting. Glaswegians, and the McCraes in particular, were not like that. There would be no kissing, no hugging, and no tears. What there was though hardly seemed adequate: these conventional words and cautious smiles.

'I never expected to see you here, Margaret.'

'And I never expected to be here, Elspeth. I wouldn't have been either if it hadn't been for Willie.'

'He always was a useful wee man.'

She's making fun of me again, thought Willie, but not maliciously.

'I've always found him so,' said Maggie.

He made himself useful then, filling a basin with warm water and taking it into Elspeth's room, where he left Maggie giving herself "a good wash".

'I don't think you should stay here, William,' said Elspeth. 'For Margaret's sake. She'll get more rest at the motel. Randolph will take you there after supper or before supper if you wish. You'll get better fare there.'

'Any time,' said Randy.

'I don't think she'll want to leave, Elspeth,' said Willie. 'She wants to be with you.'

'I have things to do, William. A sermon to prepare. Tomorrow's Sunday, you know.'

He had forgotten. Randy and he would have to wait till Monday for their trip into Holbrook for toilet paper and other luxuries.

Elspeth, he noticed, had become agitated. She was not as wholly in control of herself as he had thought. Of the two sisters she now seemed the more likely to break down.

Maggie came in, smiling.

'Margaret, I've just suggested to William that it would be better for both of you to spend the night in Holbrook and then, if you wished, return here on Monday. Tomorrow's Sunday, my busy day.'

'I'd like to stay,' said Maggie, 'but if I'm in the way I'll go.'

'You'll get more rest there. You're not well, Margaret.'

'Neither are you, Elspeth. That's why I'd like to stay.'

'Where will you sleep?'

'In that wee room in the church.'

'I don't like the church being used as a bedroom.'

'I'm sorry.'

'And there's no bed for William.'

'A blanket on the floor will do me,' he said.

The sisters stared at each other. Tears appeared in Elspeth's eyes. She did not, though, rush into Maggie's arms, nor did Maggie rush into hers.

Willie had a feeling that there was someone else in the room. He felt it so strongly that he kept turning his head to see who it was. Mrs McCrae, their mother? But how could an old woman buried many years ago in Janefield Cemetery thousands of miles away be in the room? Well, the idea of her could be. Both sisters, although so unlike each other, had a resemblance to their mother. In that way Mrs McCrae could be said to be there.

Maggie went forward. She took Elspeth's hand and pressed it against her cheek. 'Remember the last time I did that? When they told us mother was dead.'

Elspeth burst into tears and freeing her hand, rushed off to her room.

Willie put his arm round Maggie but said nothing. He could have said that Elspeth was looking back to her memories of Glasgow as much as forward to her prospects of heaven, but it would have sounded spiteful and he certainly was not feeling spiteful.

'I'm all right, Willie,' said Maggie.

He was afraid she would go after Elspeth, which he thought would have been a mistake, but no, she busied herself with the final preparations for the meal. He noticed though how her lips trembled.

9

Supper was not long delayed. Elspeth soon returned, composed again.

Though, to be candid, it was almost a paupers' meal, again mostly out of cans. Elspeth said a grace fit for a banquet. Willie judged it by its length and earnestness, for it was spoken in Navajo. He wondered why. It couldn't be that she was showing off, though he would have liked to think she was: people were never more human than when showing off. Did she think God would listen more attentively if she used the language of the cheated and doomed people? Why not? Willie himself would have if he'd been God.

'Well, William,' she said, 'you promised to tell me how you managed to raise the money to come here.'

Yes, but since then it had occurred to him that she might not be pleased, in fact might be greatly offended, by the publicity given her by the Glasgow newspaper. Maggie, he knew, had brought a cutting of the article.

'Well, William?'

'I don't think you'll be interested, Elspeth.'

'But I am, very interested. You mentioned something about your neighbours.'

Would she, as surely to God she should, be pleased to hear of the generosity of ordinary folk? It should more than make up for making public her own misfortunes; which Willie now saw had been an impertinence on all their parts.

He looked at Maggie. She understood his predicament. She nodded, giving her support.

'Weel, it was Charlie McCann's idea.'

'Charlie McCann? Should I remember him?'

'I don't ken, but everybody in the district knew Charlie. He was a street-sweeper a' his working days. His wife dee'd when he was twenty-five, having a wean; it dee'd too. He never remarried.'

'I called him a smelly old baboon,' said Maggie, 'but not to his face. I shouldn't have. I was wrong. He lives by himself.'

'Except for his cat,' said Willie. 'He's got a bad back and cannae wear socks because he cannae bend to pu' them on.'

Suddenly Willie felt a great pang of sorrow, or was it despair? No, not despair, for there was in it all the pity he was capable of. Not just for Charlie, or for Elspeth, or for Maggie; for the whole damned shooting-match. Being the kind of person he was he couldn't express it with an outburst of tears or curses. He just sat with a forkful of baked beans at his mouth, while the others waited for him to go on speaking. He felt like jumping up and rushing out into the desert and there do what? Shake his fist at the stars? Howl at them? In appeal or anger? To whom or what?

He put the beans into his mouth and chewed carefully, minding his manners.

'Well, Charlie thought that if a public appeal was made folk would be glad to contribute. The Willie Hogg Travel Fund he ca'd it. It needed publicity, so he got a reporter to put an article in a newspaper.'

'What newspaper?'

'The Glasgow Daily Chronicle.'

'You remember, Elspeth, mother used to read it.'

'Does it not go in for sensational headlines?'

'Sensational maybe,' said Willie, 'but no' scurrilous. It's a family paper.'

'Did it mention in the article what was the purpose of your journey?'

'It had to do that.'

'So I was mentioned?'

Inwardly Willie groaned. Outwardly he smiled, apologetically. 'I'm afraid so, Elspeth, but very respectfully.'

'You didn't by any chance bring a copy of the article with you?'

What did he want Maggie to do? Tell the truth and be asked to produce the article? Or lie, and keep it hidden away.

'I brought a copy,' she said.

'May I see it?' asked Elspeth.

'Of course. I've brought you a present too.'

Maggie got up to go for them. They were in her suitcase in Elspeth's room.

'I don't suppose, William,' said Elspeth, 'that it occurred to you I might not wish to be portrayed, even in a Glasgow newspaper, as a kind of freak?'

Surely she hadn't been portrayed as a freak, but as a woman of enterprise, courage, and faith.

'It wasn't like that, Elspeth,' he said, and then remembered the headline GLASGOW WOMAN AMONG REDSKINS. The truth was he hadn't given enough thought to Elspeth's part in the drama. Her life here as a missionary had been cheapened and he had been partly to blame.

Maggie came back. She had already unwrapped the souvenir plate with its scenes of Glasgow. 'Look, Elspeth. The Art Galleries. Willie sometimes goes there to look at the pictures. The People's Palace. I remember going there with you once. The University. Kelvingrove Park. Do you remember the swans?'

'It's lovely, Margaret. Thank you very much. Where is the cutting?'

Maggie handed it to her. 'People who knew you in the old days, Elspeth, were very proud of you when they read it.'

So they had been, most of them, though some had remembered her as "a haughty big bitch."

'Just bear in mind,' muttered Willie, 'it was the only way for Maggie to get to come to see you.'

'Yes.' That was all Elspeth said as, having read it carefully, she handed the cutting back to Maggie, who put it carefully in her apron pocket.

'I've been thinking,' said Maggie. 'Tomorrow's Sunday. Will there
be a service in the church?'

There was, Willie saw, purpose in her apparent naïvety.

'Yes,' said Elspeth.

'Did you know it's awfully dusty?'

'Yes, I knew.'

'I don't suppose you believe in people working on Sundays?'

'No, I don't.'

'Right. Willie and me will go over now and give it a good cleaning.'

She wasn't being obtuse, Willie saw. She was keeping Elspeth's
mind on religion and therefore on forgiveness. 'I'm looking forward
to it,' she said. 'The service, I mean.'

'There is no need for you and William to attend.'

'Oh, we wouldn't miss it for the world. Would we, Willie?'

He shook his head.

'It is not an entertainment, Margaret.'

'I know that.'

'It is conducted in Navajo. Therefore you will not understand a
word of it.'

'That'll not stop us enjoying it.'

Elspeth looked as if she was about to condemn the use of the word
but thought better of it. Were not worshippers meant to enjoy communion with God?

'Don't you approve of visitors, Elspeth?' he asked.

'Not if they come to mock.'

'Willie would never do that,' said Maggie. 'He's not a believer
himself but he respects people who are. Don't you, Willie?'

Her prattling was deliberate. The alternative was for them all to sit
in bitter silence.

'We'll all go,' said Maggie. 'Won't we, Mr Hansen?'

He shook his head. 'Sorry, Mrs Hogg. Count me out.'

If she was my wife, thought Willie, I'd attend all her services, though
I think I'm as determined an atheist as he is. I'd hand out the
hymn-books, I'd sweep the floor, I'd play the piano, I'd throw out any
who came drunk. I wouldn't think I was betraying my principles.
Anyway I hope I would always put my wife before my principles.

'Well, at least you'll not object to helping Willie and me sweeping
out the church. After we've done the dishes we'll all go over. You go

and lie down, Elspeth. I'll come in later and we'll have a long blether, just the two of us.'

'Aye, you do that, Elspeth,' said Willie, cheerfully.

They stared at each other, old adversaries, the tall woman obsessed with religion, the small man with his blithe disbelief.

'Don't just stand there, Willie,' said Maggie. 'There's work to be done.'

He felt he had to make closer contact with Elspeth, so he patted her on the shoulder, as a football player might have done to a colleague who had just scored a brilliant goal.

It was thin, her shoulder. He felt the bones. He remembered the plump shoulders of her youth. He had never touched them then. What if he had married her, instead of Maggie? What if he had come to America all those years ago? Life would have been more exciting but would it have been any more fruitful? Was it possible that while he was courting Maggie he and Elspeth had been fancying each other? She had often been scornful but that could have been a pretence. She had been as handsome a young woman as he had ever met: those proud breasts, that ample behind, those fierce blue eyes.

You're kidding yourself, Willie Hogg, he said to himself, as he took his place by the sink. It was never on. She saw you as a wee gallus Glesca keelie. She thought you weren't good enough even for Maggie.

10

The dishes done, and the church dusted and tidied, Maggie said she was going across to the house to have the long-awaited blether with her sister.

'Are you no' too tired?' asked Willie. 'Can't you wait till the morrow?'

'Are you forgetting we haven't seen each other for thirty-eight years? Thirty-eight!'

What advice should he give her? Don't make it too long. Remember she's tired and ill and in pain. She'll want to prepare her mind for tomorrow's service. She's disappointed with her man. She'll not be in a mood to listen to Glasgow gossip, about people she knew long ago and has forgotten, about buildings that have been knocked down and shops that have disappeared. She never had much patience with that kind of gossip, less now than ever. Don't stay longer than ten minutes. Don't ask why she's never had any children. And don't run down your father.

But it would have been impertinent of him to offer her any advice at all. So he just said: 'I'll go and have a chat with Randy. See you in aboot ten minutes.'

'Och, I'll need a lot longer than that.'

'There's always the morrow. She needs rest, Maggie, and so do you.'

Randy was in his hidey-hole with Mozart and a bottle of Cutty Sark. He made Willie welcome.

For a minute or two they were silent, listening to the music and sipping the whisky.

'How long have you been married, Randy?'

'Fifteen years.'

So he and Elspeth had both been middle-aged.

'Me and Maggie, forty-seven years.'

There was another silence.

'Was she religious then?'

'She was.'

'Were you a believer yourself?'

'No.'

So why did you marry her? Could it be you were so much in love that God did not matter? Willie knew that he ought to shut up, it was none of his business; but he was too interested.

'Did you get married in church?' he asked.

'We did.'

'Maggie and me were married by declaration. We just declared in front of witnesses that we regarded oorselves as married. No minister. No church. An old Scottish custom. Since abolished by Parliament.'

'Was that what Maggie wanted?'

'It must have been for she didn't object.'

'That doesn't follow, does it?'

'No, it doesn't. As a matter of fact she likes weddings, you know, white dress, flowers, music.'

'Most women do.'

Maggie often stood at the entrance to a church to throw confetti even when the bride was a stranger. Had he selfishly and meanly deprived her of one of the greatest joys in life for a woman? Her mother had chided him. Elspeth had often cast it up. Maggie, though, never had.

'We'll hae a golden wedding to make up for it,' he said. 'If we live long enough and if we can afford it.'

'Another William Hogg Fund called for?'

Through a small window they could see the stars. Willie had never seen them so bright. He imagined he could feel the earth turning as it hurtled through space. In a place like this any man with imagination was an astronaut. He should have felt humble in the midst of such gigantic and mysterious forces, but he did not. There was no love out there.

'Magnificent,' he said. 'The stars here.'

'Do they make you feel insignificant?'

'Weel no, I've just been thinking they didn't. Whit are they? Enormous balls of fire. I'd rather have the lizard I saw sunning itself on a stone.' And Maggie meant immeasurably more to him.

He wondered, rather uneasily, what she and Elspeth were talking about.

'Elspeth,' he said, and took a sip of whisky.

Randy waited.

'She's amazing. Do the Indians respect her? Do they really want her to be here?'

'I am not the person to ask that, Willie.'

'Missionaries often go where they're not wanted. They often do more harm than good. The Indians have their own religion, haven't they? The Great Spirit. The Happy Hunting Ground. As you said, the harmonious relationship with nature.'

Randy was still dourly silent.

'You don't want to talk about this, Randy?'

'No.'

'Well, do you mind if I talk about Maggie and me?'

'If you want someone to listen, Willie, I'll listen gladly.'

'Thanks. You see, I've just made a discovery: I love her. A bit late in the day, you might think, after knowing her for fifty years. Not a discovery, really. More like an admission. I used to tell myself I was fond of her and wanted to look efter her. But that was a'. Mind you, you could spend your entire life in Glesca withoot hearing onybody utter the word love. We're no' that kind o' people. We keep sich things to oorselves. To tell you the truth I didn't think she was worthy o' me.'

'I don't think you need reproach yourself, Willie. You may have had doubts but Maggie never has. She thinks you love her, Willie, and always have done.'

'You think so?'

'It's as plain as the nose on your face.'

'Which is plain enough.'

'Listen to the music, Willie. Mozart says it all, better than we ever could.'

Yes, the music was eloquent and consoling and perhaps it did give his thoughts about Maggie a dignity and resonance that they might not otherwise have had.

What were Maggie's religious beliefs? He just did not know. She never spoke about them and he had not thought it worth asking. If she thought she had done someone wrong she would impose a penance on herself, such as doing without sugar in her tea if the offence had been small, or handing in some possession she valued to the Oxfam shop if it was great. She would no more think of talking about the cysts that sometimes afflicted her than about God. She had once told him she did not believe in heaven—though she wasn't sure about hell—and yet at the grave in Janefield Cemetery she talked to her mother. No woman could have been less of a feminist and yet she had once startled him by being indignant about the way men assumed that God was male.

'Weel, thanks for the hospitality,' he said, rising. 'I'll have to go and see how Maggie's getting on.'

'Is she on medication, Willie?'

'She takes pills for her heart. Why?'

'She seems to catch her breath now and then, as if she was in pain.'

'She's been told to take it easy.'

Maggie was still in Elspeth's room. He knocked on the door. She came to it.

'Time for bed, hen. Will I carry across a pot of hot water?'

'If you wouldn't mind, Willie.'

She shut the door again and went back in to her sister. It was childish of him, but he felt left out and jealous.

He went to the kitchen and heated water. The supply was getting low. Randy and he were going tomorrow morning to replenish it.

There were cushions on the living-room chairs. He gathered some for him to sleep on. Randy had found him a blanket.

He knocked at the door again. Maggie took her time in coming. He heard one of the old women snorting in her sleep.

Maggie was still dry-eyed. She was so pleased to see him that tears almost came into his own eyes. How stupid he had been to feel jealous.

'Have you taken your pills today?' he asked, anxiously.

'Don't fuss, Willie.'

But in the living-room she swallowed them while he watched.

'Do you feel any pain?' he asked.

'Pain?'

'Aye.'

'Don't be silly. Everybody feels pain. She's not happy about us sleeping in the church, Willie, but I told her that when a disaster like an earthquake strikes a country churches are used to give people shelter.'

He wondered what else she had told her sister. Perhaps she would tell him one day, when they were back in Glasgow.

They went out into the chilly starlight.

'I have to pay a call, Willie.'

'I'll wait here.'

In a minute or so she rejoined him and they went into the church together.

11

Next morning they were all up early. Randy and Willie had to go with the truck to fetch water, Elspeth having given them special dispensation. In any case Willie hadn't slept well because of the hardness of the floor and the bumpiness of the cushions; they had also stunk. Maggie, though, had had a good night's rest, or so she said. She had had one of her "Nice" dreams for a change. She and Willie had been living in a wigwam. They had adopted a baby, called Beatrice, after his mother. She didn't know what happened after that for she had woken up.

After breakfast Randy and Willie set off. On their way they saw, beside the road, on a small hill, an old white-haired Indian sitting cross-legged. He would have been there all night, said Randy, in a stupor if you wanted to use a contemptuous word or a trance if you felt charitable. He wouldn't be drunk, at least not with hooch. He was communing with the Great Spirit. He would be intoning an endless song.

Willie was reminded of a visit he and Charlie McCann had paid to a friend Jack Cairncross in hospital. Poor Jack had taken a stroke which had caused massive damage to his brain. He was paralysed and doubly incontinent. A child of two would have recognised them; he could not. They had held his hand and told him what a splendid day it was outside but they had been talking to themselves. Afterwards in the *Airlie Arms* they had angrily agreed that Jack should be given a pill to end his degradation. It was abominable hypocrisy of society to approve of bombs that could kill millions and yet refuse, on the grounds that life was sacred, to help an old man to die with dignity.

Depression struck him, like heartburn.

'You ken, Randy, I get disgusted at times,' he said.

Randy smiled. 'You surprise me, Willie. I've been thinking you're the most radiant man I've ever met.'

'Radiant?'

'Sure.'

'Weel, I often don't feel radiant. How many come to Elspeth's services?'

'It varies. The average is about fifteen. But there should be a full turn-out today.'

'Why?'

'Because of the truck that's coming from San Diego.'

'With the offerings?'

'Right.'

'Don't tell me they've been warned that if they don't come to church they won't get anything.'

'Such hints have been dropped.'

Willie was disappointed. That was what the Salvation Army would have done. Sing a hymn or you won't get your bowl of soup. He hadn't thought Elspeth would be so petty. But perhaps she was under orders from higher up.

'That's treating them as if they were weans or paupers.'

'They are looked upon as paupers. But how would you divide the offerings, Willie?'

'Weel, I'd try to make it depend on need and not how often you attended church.'

'But don't you agree that some people are more deserving than others?'

'Deserving?' It was a word Willie distrusted. Once when he had been expounding his socialist utopia Charlie McCann had asked: 'Whit aboot the lazy bastards that let everybody else dae a' the work?'

'Yes, Willie. Deserving.'

Randy was able to be so philosophical because he had given up not only on God but on mankind too. He was free to scoff. The more injustices there were, and the more feeble the efforts to remedy them, the more freely he could sneer and laugh. There was something Beelzebubian about that small white beard.

'Is the wilderness finding you out, Willie?'

'Whit do you mean?'

'In the wilderness a man empties his mind and sets the contents in front of him, just as he might empty his pockets for the police. He sees what a pitiable collection of petty thoughts and hackneyed beliefs he has, not one remotely original. So he shoves them all back in again and returns to society no wiser but not any less self-satisfied.'

'And that's whit's happening to me?'

'It's what happens to us all. There are few exceptions. I can think only of one.'

'And who's that?'

'Maggie.'

'Maggie? My Maggie?'

'Yes. Your Maggie, Willie. A woman utterly without pretensions. Therefore, without a scrap of phoniness. We clever fellows look for answers and pretend we find them. Phonies, every one of us. Do you think that old woman would have given us her necklace? Never in a thousand years. And did you see how beautifully Maggie accepted it?'

This praise of Maggie pleased Willie, but was it sincere? Was Beelzebub taking the mickey? Yet, though Maggie's views were often peculiar it was true they were never smug or phony, as the old Indian women, guided by instinct, had recognised.

12

In helping to get Elspeth ready for the service in the afternoon Maggie was as happy as a little girl playing a game. Ignoring Elspeth's protests she polished her sister's shoes and replaced a worn lace. She discovered a tear in the black gown and sewed it, meticulously. Then she pressed the gown, with the old-fashioned flatiron. She insisted then on "doing" Elspeth's hair, washing it and then setting it. She had always wanted to be a hairdresser, she said. Did Elspeth remember that? Did she notice her sister's frequent winces? Willie wondered for she gave no sign, until once, when Elspeth was out of the room, she remarked: 'You know, she'll not even take an aspirin.' Whether it was simply an observation or a criticism of Elspeth's stubbornness or praise of Elspeth's faith Willie could not say. Maggie had secrets which even he was not to be told.

Willie had often maintained in the *Airlie Arms* and elsewhere, and had been good-humouredly barracked for it, that he had never met anyone who had wholly convinced him that he or she truly believed in God. Army chaplains, one with a major's crowns on his shoulders; Catholic priests from the mystic bogs of Ireland; Church of Scotland ministers; ladies who helped in Oxfam shops; nuns collecting for St Vincent de Paul; short-haired Mormons offering free pamphlets; Pakistanis on their knees four times a day and bereaved husbands and wives: none had passed the test. Most had been decent people, reasonably charitable towards their fellow man but the fire in the soul, which would have set Willie's own alight, dampened though his was with a life-time of incredulity, had been missing. A famous American evangelist had once descended on Glasgow to bring sinners back to Christ. Thousands had rushed to hear his ranting addresses. Dozens had gone forward, some on their knees, to give themselves to their Saviour; but none, especially the wild-eyed preacher himself, had struck Willie as being divinely inspired. Indeed, atheistic himself, he had resented the way the conception of God had been abused. A great deal of money had changed hands. He had gone home peeved and disappointed. What had Maggie's pertinent comment been? 'They say he's got his ain jet-plane, that one.'

But had he now met someone who might pass the test? That she was his sister-in-law and had been born in a two-room-and kitchen in the Cowcaddens hardly disqualified her. Hadn't Christ been born in a stable? He had been made aware of the joy she felt but he had not been able to share it. He had suspected it might be a bizarre consequence of the cancer destroying her body. At the service this afternoon he might find out. It could be the most important event in his life.

How would the worshippers come? he asked Randy.

By pick-up truck, dilapidated jalopy, donkey, or on foot. Some would walk ten miles and the same back.

Did Willie know what a somnambulist was? Willie did. Well, he'd see plenty of them that afternoon.

It turned out to be no exaggeration. After two they began to arrive, crowded into trucks or old sagging cars. Two came on donkeys. There were women and children, all sombrely dressed and with stolid faces. The church was soon packed. Maggie whispered that she had never seen such well-behaved children. Not even babies in arms cried. Willie did not notice a single smile. His own smiles evoked no response. But then, to be fair, if this had been a church service of the Wee Free Kirk in Scotland, in the Hebrides say, he would not have seen any smiles either, for to those bigots communion with Jehovah was a grim business. But these Indians were not merely unsmiling, they were soaked in solemnity; even toddlers with ribbons in their hair.

The leaders of the chapter, Mr Simpson and Mr McKellar, with their families, came in late and sat in the front row, where Maggie and Willie had intended to sit. Instead they had to sit on chairs behind the lectern, facing the congregation. It had the disadvantage that Elspeth would have her back to them and Willie had wanted to watch her face.

Punctually at three according to Willie's Timex Elspeth came in, neatly dressed in the black gown from neck to ankles. Thanks to Maggie her shoes shone. With her white face and whiter hair she reminded Willie of someone back from the dead in a horror film; except that the expression on her face could never have been achieved by any actress, however skilful and highly paid. Unbearable pain and unbearable faith were stamped on it. If she had suddenly collapsed Willie wouldn't have been surprised. He got ready to rush forward and help.

She held herself straight, with a conscious effort, as drunkards did, and walked with slow deliberation to the lectern, where she held up her hand in blessing. Willie could not see her face, which meant he might miss the moment of truth after all, if it ever came. A bluebottle buzzed in the silence. Maggie sighed. Outside a creature screamed. A dog barked. Was God here, in this cheap church, in the person of this sick tormented woman in the black gown?

He felt tingles, in his hands, his scalp, and his testicles. It had nothing to do with sexual attraction. He had never felt anything of that kind for Elspeth, even when she was young and desirable. What did these tingles mean? Was he one of those rare persons sensitive to supernatural presences? Beside him Maggie was smiling at a little Indian girl in the front row.

But surely he should be feeling something more than these tingles. They could after all be caused by belated cramp, after his night on the hard floor or the bumpy ride in the truck. He felt more hopeful for humanity than he had done earlier but his pessimism then had been uncharacteristic; it was his nature to be hopeful, if not radiant. To be truthful, he had felt just as uplifted at Firhill Park when Partick Thistle had scored a goal.

Where was that lowe in the soul, burning away all doubts?

Elspeth was now at the piano playing the opening notes of a hymn. She sang it too and some of the congregation joined in, though not rollickingly as the tune required, but mournfully. It was the children's hymn "What a Friend We Have In Jesus", though the words were in Navajo. Willie felt disconcerted. He remembered when he was a small boy sneaking into the Band of Hope and joining in jolly hymns denouncing strong drink. Here he was, waiting for his soul to be set on fire, and they were singing "What a Friend We Have in Jesus", not joyfully but as if they all expected to be hurled into hell. There was going to be no sign, no fire in the soul. Whether the fault was his, in that he was not receptive enough, or God's, in that either He didn't exist or didn't want anything to do with humanity, remained an open question.

Maggie was singing, in English but she didn't seem sure of the words.

Elspeth then read from the Bible. Though it was in Navajo he recognised the passage: the parable of the loaves and fishes. Maggie had once said to him the fish must have been herring. 'It's the only fish, Willie, you've got mair of at the finish than at the start.'

They sang another hymn: "Jesus loves me".

At the Band of Hope you were given an orange or an apple when leaving. Here they were promised all kinds of goodies, to be doled out tomorrow.

After the sermon, which did not last long – Elspeth was already exhausted – she reminded them, in Navajo and English, of the consignment of goods coming from San Diego tomorrow. They would be distributed on Tuesday.

For the first time they showed interest. They wanted to know more. They muttered among themselves. They appealed to their headmen. Who was to get what?

Elspeth hardly made it to the anteroom.

Willie and Maggie went out to watch the worshippers depart.

'Well, Maggie, what did you think of the service?'

She did not seem to hear him. 'She was saying she'd like to pay us a visit in Glasgow this summer. I said she'd be very welcome.'

'Of course she would, but, Maggie – '

'I know it's not possible. So does she. She knows she's going to die. It could be today or tomorrow.'

He was taken aback by that calm acceptance, not on Elspeth's part but on Maggie's.

'Wouldn't she be better then in hospital?' he said.

'What do you mean better?'

'Weel, mair comfortable.'

'She's not looking for comfort. She's long past wanting comfort.'

Yes, Maggie, but what is it she wants? Did she tell you? Did you understand? The old Maggie never would have. This rediscovered Maggie evidently did.

'I'll go and see how she is,' she said.

'I'll go wi' you.'

'No, Willie.'

'No' ? Why no' ?'

'She's not sure of you.'

'Whit do you mean?'

'She thinks you're laughing at her, trying to convert these heathens.'

'But you ken I'm no' laughing at her. Didn't you tell her?'

'I don't always know what you're thinking, Willie. You don't tell me, you know.'

'Weel, I'll tell you this, I feel mair like weeping.'

'She'd think that worse than laughing at her.'

Bewildered and miserable, he stood and watched Maggie as she went back into the church.

How could you live with another person for nearly fifty years and not know her? He had thought there might be riches in her but he had not made enough effort to discover them. He had never valued her as he should. In the few years they had left together could he make it up to her?

He heard music from Randy's hut. He did not want to go there. Perhaps he should wander far off into the desert and find out just how limited his resources were, moral as well as intellectual.

Suddenly he became aware of an old man, an Indian, gazing at him from the gable of the church. He had long white hair and wore a black jacket and a black bowler: just the garb for a kirk elder. But Willie did not remember seeing him among the congregation. Perhaps he had arrived too late.

He seemed to be signalling to Willie with his stick but whatever the message was there was no hurry. All round them was eternity, so what did a minute matter or a week or a year?

Willie walked over to him. 'Hello,' he said.

The old man frowned. This was rushing the acquaintance. 'Hi' he replied, after about twenty champs of his leathery jaws.

'Were you too late for the service?'

'I not go to damn service.'

So why was he here? Where had he come from? He must have walked. All the vehicles were gone.

The old man pointed to himself. 'Joe,' he said.

Willie did likewise. 'Willie. Would you like a glass of water, Joe?'

'How old?' asked Joe, again pointing to himself.

About a hundred and fifty, thought Willie, but he said, 'Ninety.'

'Ninety-two.'

Could he be the husband of one of Elspeth's crones, come to see how she was?

He poked Willie in the chest. 'You will get me a bed.'

'A bed?'

'When the truck comes. I got no bed.'

Well, as a matter of fact, Joe, I haven't got a bed either. But it would have been childish to say it.

'You get me a bed.'

How to explain that he had no authority? But he could at least discuss it with Randy and perhaps Elspeth if she felt able. If Joe was really ninety-two he certainly ought to have a bed, even if he hadn't gone to the "damn" service.

Joe then began to walk off into the desert, in the direction of the red bluffs. Willie could make out no habitation there.

He went to consult Randy.

'Joe? He lives about six miles away. By himself. He claims to be descended from Manuelito, a famous Navajo chief who surrendered in 1868, I think it was. He says he has never surrendered himself.'

'But he was cadging a bed!'

'You think that inconsistent with his attitude of no surrender?'

'Well, isn't it? Will he get a bed?'

'He never attends church, so he doesn't qualify.'

'Surely Elspeth wouldn't hold that against someone who's ninety-two?'

'She wouldn't but his compatriots would. Why should they have to endure church-going, while he gets away with skipping it?'

'Is that all church-going means to them?'

'To most of them.'

Willie felt depressed, for Elspeth's sake. 'I think I'll go for a walk,' he said.

'Would you like me to come with you?'

'If you don't mind, Randy, I'd rather be alone.'

But he wasn't alone. The old mangy dog followed at his heels.

13

When Willie was allowed at last to see Elspeth she was in her own room and in her own bed, with Maggie the nurse in attendance, and the three old Indian women crooning a song.

It was, Elspeth explained in a hoarse voice, about the daughter of a chief who had been killed in an accident with a runaway mustang. Not very appropriate, she added, with a smile: the girl was young and beautiful, and the horse swift.

Willie continued to be amazed and humbled by Maggie's competence and tact. She let the old women finish their dirge and then took them away to prepare food for them.

Elspeth looked up at him. Every now and then she grimaced involuntarily. She seemed older than the women who had just gone out.

'Well, William, what did you think of the service?'

He had to be very careful. 'The congregation could have been mair co-operative.'

'I'm afraid I haven't yet won their complete trust.'

'Considering their history, it would seem impossible.'

After all those who had dispossessed them had carried Bibles as well as guns.

'Some of the women, without their men, have shown me trust.'

'An old man was talking to me after the rest had gone. He hadn't been to the service. Joe, he said his name was. He gave his age as ninety-two. He asked me if I could get him a bed.'

'He does not approve of me.'

'But will he get his bed, if there's one to spare?'

'That could be up to you, William.'

'Me?'

'Yes. You may have to supervise the distribution, if I am not able.'

'Shouldn't Randy do that?'

'He won't want to be involved. I have made a list which might help you.'

'Won't they object to taking orders from me?'

'I'm sure, William, they have heard of Glasgow's reputation for fair-mindedness.'

He was pleased to hear her making fun of him, though it almost had him in tears.

'You must be very proud of Margaret,' she said.

'Aye.'

'We weren't fair to her.'

'Weel, I wasn't, often.'

'I used to be so impatient with her.'

'We all were.'

'Now she's an example to us all. So serene.'

'Serene?' Aye, it was the right word.

'But she is not well herself. She turns pale so suddenly.'

'She's had heart trouble for some time. She takes pills for it.'

His own heart missed several beats. Surely Maggie was in no serious danger.

'Look after her, William.'

'I'll dae my best.'

She closed her eyes. 'Would you believe me, William, if I was to tell you that this pain has become a comfort to me, even when I have felt I could bear it no longer?'

Aye, Elspeth, I could believe you and I've got enough imagination to know what you mean.

'It is not for His creatures to question God's purpose,' she said.

That was something often discussed in the *Airlie Arms*: God's purpose; with as much pertinence and a lot more wit than in a theological college. He himself had pointed out how the human mind was slippery with—what was the word?—casuistry. (They had teased him for it.) It could escape from any philosophical impasse with the ease of a Houdini. God's purpose could be found in everything, from AIDS to the deaths by starvation of thousands of black children. In the one case it was to punish homosexuals, and in the other to test the compassion of Christians.

Again he said nothing.

'Would you please tell Randolph I would like to see him?'

'Sure.' Yet he hesitated. Randy had let drop that he couldn't bear to see her suffer. Suppose it was Maggie lying there with her skull showing through the skin and her body shrinking back from the agony, would he be able to bear it?

'I'll go noo and tell him.'

He found Maggie outside, on the doorstep, with a blanket over her shoulders. At first he thought she was weeping, but she was really gasping for breath.

'It's the air in this place, Willie, it's so thin I can scarcely breathe.'

He felt great alarm. 'It's cauld too. Elspeth wants to see Randy. I'm going to tell him. Are you remembering to take your pills?'

'I'm fine now. I'll make some tea.'

Maggie's panacea, a cup of tea. But it was the human companionship it represented that she had faith in, and what better thing was there?

'She wants to see you, Randy.'

'What's happening, Willie?'

'She's in bed. She's all right. Christ no, she's not all right. Maybe whit I mean is that she's reconciled.'

'To what? To going into hospital?'

'No, not that.'

'Can't you and Maggie persuade her?'

'I'm no' sure we want to. You see, she knows, and we know, that she's going to die very soon, it could be today or tomorrow.'

'Well?'

'Right. So it's a bit late to talk about hospital. I've got naething against hospitals. I worked in one for forty years and had naething but admiration for the doctors, nurses, and staff. I saw lots of people die there. I'll likely die in a hospital myself.'

'What are you trying to say, Willie?'

'Deeing in a hospital's no' for Elspeth. Here, in this desert, is where she wants to dee and where she should dee.'

'Does Maggie think that too?'

'She does. So, are you coming? Just haud her hand, that's a'.'

An impassioned, almost angry note, came into Randy's voice. 'I have to say this, Willie, and you're the only person I could say it to. For the past five years I have been treated with contempt and neglect.'

Willie felt desolate. 'Strong words, Randy.'

'Yet I have come here voluntarily to help if I could and – this is not a boast – I have never spoken a single word in recrimination.'

You've often not spoken at all, Randy.

'She's been ill, Randy, very ill. Worse than that, she's been afraid that she's been wasting her time here. It's hard for you and me to understand, but for a believer to feel that God has turned His back must be harder to bear than cancer.'

Randy took Willie's hand. 'You're a good man, Willie Hogg. Give me a minute and I'll be over.'

'Good. Maggie should have the tea ready by then.'

Maggie not only had the tea ready, she served it, on a tray, in elegant cups and saucers that she found at the back of a cupboard: more wedding presents never before used. It struck Willie that the scene in Elspeth's little room would have made a good subject for a painter, one talented enough to catch the pathos underlying ordinary things. A favourite refuge of his at home was the Glasgow Art Galleries which he often visited to refresh his spirit. He had once invited his *Airlie Arms* cronies to accompany him. Standing in front of a Rembrandt self-portrait in old age, Alec McDougall had remarked: 'You ken, Willie, he's no' unlike you.' The others, much amused, had seen the resemblance too: the same boozy-looking nose, raddled cheeks, sensitive mouth, and rueful truthful eyes. Perhaps they had not meant it as a compliment but he had taken it as one. Now, though he lacked the great painter's ability to portray it, he saw this scene as Rembrandt might have: the proud doomed woman in bed, her husband holding her hand with a strange awkwardness, Maggie wearing her tartan apron, and Willie himself, the eager observer, keeping out of the way. What little items would the painter have picked out? The design on the cups: small yellow flowers. Maggie's apron. The uncanny blueness of Elspeth's eyes. Randy's white beard hiding his stiff lips. Willie's own expression of earnest goodwill. Maggie's attentive hands, with the wedding ring glittering.

Next time he went to the Art Galleries he would imagine that painting among all the others. He would peer at the signature at the bottom. W. Hogg.

14

The truck from San Diego arrived at the Mission early on Tuesday morning; it had spent the night in Holbrook. Willie had expected a lorry of some size, for it seemed donations had been accumulating for weeks, but what appeared outside the church, dwarfing it indeed, was enormous, consisting not of one huge pantechnicon but two joined together. The driver of this monster was a tall fair-haired man wearing a baseball cap, who soon demonstrated by his language – he used "goddamn" frequently – that he was not a church member himself; he was simply an employee of the trucking company that was lending the rig for the purpose. His assistants, though, who were to unload the trucks, were God-loving, clean-shaven, short-haired, young evangelicals who as they staggered about, steadfast as ants, burdened with heavy and awkward articles of furniture, kept exhorting one another with cries of 'Praise the Lord!' or 'Hosannah!' or – though this was used less enthusiastically as the day wore on – "A burden for the Lord is as a feather."

Willie started out by thinking them insufferable, then he saw them as comic, and ended up by finding them still comic but admirable.

They had travelled hundreds of miles in much discomfort and were exhausting, not to say bruising, themselves in the service of strangers, semi-heathens at that, and looked for no other reward than the Lord's approbation.

Since Elspeth wasn't able and Randy was reluctant Willie had to take on the job of chief distributor. For weeks Elspeth had been compiling a list of families, with the articles needed or requested by them. He had everything arranged in separate piles, beds in one, clothing in another, and so on, to make the sharing out next day easier. The young porters made jokes about his accent and called him Grandpaw but heeded his instructions. Jocularly they confessed they were glad they would not be present tomorrow to watch the share-out. A cavalry detachment would be needed to keep order. Would it not be a good idea they suggested, this time not jesting, to hold a prayer-meeting first, in the open air, with everyone on their knees for an hour or so? Not only would the peace of the Lord be in their souls, their legs would be so cramped that they would not be able to rush forward and grab. Answering piety with irony, Willie retorted that he was depending on the sense of decency and fairness that was in everyone, especially those not corrupted by capitalist values. The young men's response was to dance in a ring round him, chanting that there was not a man with greater faith, no, not in all Israel. He could have kicked their arses but couldn't help laughing.

They could be right, though. A shotgun might be useful tomorrow, if not that night, for what was to prevent some sneaking up in the dark and helping themselves? Willie had often been astonished, not to say exasperated, by the forbearance of the poor, but here was an occasion when he hoped they would continue to forbear. He dreaded a face-scratching, hair-tugging, screaming free-for-all.

After the big vans had gone and darkness had fallen he was in the house resting when he heard car engines outside. He dashed out. There were two pick-up trucks. One was driven by Bartholomew Simpson, the other by Henry McKellar. They had their wives with them. They offered no explanation but began at once to help themselves.

He rushed at them like a terrier. They heeded his protests no more than they would have a little dog's bark. Nor were they interested in his homily on the immorality of their using their official positions to

take the best of what was available. After all it was what was done
everywhere in the world. Nevertheless he felt so incensed at their
impudence and his own impotence that he ran into the house for the
revolver he had seen in a drawer. It had no bullets in it but he could
use it to frighten off these poaching bastards.

He found Elspeth on her feet, wrapped in a blanket, ready to go
out. Maggie was holding her by the arm.

He was horrified, especially at Maggie's part in it.

'She knows what she's doing, Willie,' she said, calmly. 'It's her duty.
She was expecting this.'

What was the use of saying that she was shortening her life?

Assisted by Maggie and Willie himself, Elspeth went out, proud as
a queen. She approached the marauders. They stopped what they were
doing. They knew that she was close to death. It could be the Great
Spirit speaking through her. She addressed them in their own language, not angrily but with a grave authority. They could not bear to
look at her. Willie waited for them to ignore her, like sulky children, and
resume filling their trucks, but no, sulkily indeed, they began to return
what they had taken. She did not wait till they had replaced it all but
turned and went back into the house, helped by Maggie. Willie expected
a burst of contemptuous laughter and a resumption of the looting, but
there was silence, except for a mutter of regret from one of the women
who perhaps had had her heart set on something in particular.

Soon the two vehicles were on their way again, into the darkness,
empty.

It looked as if Elspeth had not been wasting her time at the Mission.

Later, as Willie and Maggie, were about to go over to the church
where they slept Maggie made a suggestion that, though very sensible,
almost demoralised him. Why should he at his age lie on lumpy
cushions on a hard floor when there were at least a dozen beds in good
condition within reach? She had noticed one in particular; the mattress
had looked quite new. If there wasn't space in the little room where
her own bed was he could sleep in the church itself.

'But, Maggie, I cannae dae that after chasing that lot away.'

'Don't be silly. You could put it back in the morning and nobody
would know. Or you could keep it for that old man of ninety-two who
spoke to you.'

'I've got nae rights here, Maggie. I'm just a visitor.'

'A visitor that's made himself very useful. You deserve a good rest. And I'm not having you go home, Willie Hogg, with a bad back. If anybody objects, blame me. I'll know what to say to them. Get Mr Hansen to help you.'

So, with Willie still mumbling, they went to Randy and found him more than willing to help. Why just a bed and mattress? He had noticed an assortment of chamber pots.

'You've been drinking, Mr Hansen,' said Maggie, sternly. 'Think shame.' There was a smell of whisky off him.

'If you two bring the bed and mattress,' said Maggie, 'I'll go to the church and find a suitable place.'

Willie had to give in. 'Weel, if we're going to dae it,' he said, 'I'll sleep on your bed, Maggie, and you can have the mair comfortable one.'

'I'm not sleeping in the church.'

'Why no"

'Don't ask. I just don't want to.'

'Please yourself. We'll put the camp bed in the church for me and this ither one in the wee room for you. How's that?'

'You know, Mr Hansen, he'd rather sleep on the hard ground. Wouldn't you say that was foolish?'

'Very foolish,' said Randy.

'He's always been like that. He would never take a penny that he didn't think he was entitled to.'

What about the Fund? asked Willie, but of himself. Aloud he said. 'It's cauld oot here. You go into the church, Maggie, but don't move onything. Wait for us.'

'All right. You'll know the one I mean. The mattress has big roses all over it.'

Using a torch Willie and Randy went over to the pile of beds. They easily identified the one Maggie meant.

They carried the mattress first.

The old dog yelped in the background. It wasn't hungry, for Willie had fed it, but it was lonely, it had sores, and it could hardly walk for rheumatism in one of its legs. Yet Willie envied it. Its conscience was clear.

Later, as he lay trying to get to sleep he heard Maggie coughing. She had wanted the door of the small room kept open.

'Are you a' right, hen?' he called. 'You sound as if you're taking a cauld.'

'I'm fine. Know what I've been thinking, Willie? When we get back home I'd like to buy a new three-piece suite. That one we have is nearly thirty years old.'

He was astonished. 'Using whit for money?'

'We should have plenty left.'

'Do you mean the Fund money?'

'It's ours, isn't it? It was given to us.'

'But not to buy a three-piece suite.'

'Look at it this way, Willie. When we get back we'll be worn out, body and soul.'

'I'll no' deny that.'

'So we'll need something to give us a lift.'

'So we will.' But would even Dr Saunders prescribe a three-piece suite as a tonic?

'And it would remind us of Elspeth.'

This was the old and new Maggie combined.

One of Willie's heroes was David Hume, the Edinburgh philosopher, who at the age of twenty-seven had written his famous book *A Treatise of Human Nature*. Faced with some moral problem Willie often wondered what Hume's opinion would have been. Would Maggie's proposal have stumped him?

'Will you think about it, Willie?'

'Aye, I'll think aboot it.'

'Good night, Willie.'

'Good night, Maggie.'

They heard the dog howling outside.

Perhaps, thought Willie, with a sigh, its conscience isn't clear after all.

15

Willie got up very early, when the sky was still red with sunrise and the air still chilly. This wasn't so that he could return the purloined bed before distribution began at ten o'clock. He could hardly do that while Maggie was asleep in it and in any case he had decided to take her advice and give it to old Joe, in a day or two. No, he was up so early, when there was no one else about, because the vast loneliness and magnificence of the sky fascinated him. Also, just as good a reason, he could relieve himself with composure, if not with dignity. He did not mind the old dog watching him. It now recognised him as the one who fed it but there was more gratitude than greed in those rheumy eyes. What's going to happen to you, he asked, when the Mission closes, as it's bound to very soon. The dog whined in answer and wagged its tail. It would have licked his face if he hadn't, tactfully so as not to hurt its feelings, prevented it.

He was startled by a rattling noise. It wasn't loud enough to be made by a car or truck. Standing, and pulling up his trousers, he looked in that direction and saw, silhouetted against the bright sky, old Joe, pushing a barrow; its wheels were making the noise. He had come for his bed.

He said so, not with a beggar's cringe but with a chief's haughtiness. He did look comic and pathetic, with his bowler hat and home-made barrow, but he did not look defeated. If he had had a thousand braves in warpaint behind him he could not have been more confident in his cause; which was, alas, the right to a bed and not to a great prairie full of buffalo.

Would he, Willie wondered, be satisfied with the camp bed? It folded up and so was easily portable. The mattress that went with it was very thin, as Willie's bones knew. Still, he could at least offer it.

He went into the church, stealthily, so as not to waken Maggie, folded up the camp bed, mattress and all, and carried it out.

Joe, or Thundercloud, which, according to Randy had been his Indian name, gave it a scornful glance and then pushed his barrow to the pile of beds where he picked out one more suitable for a chief. As Willie watched, reluctant to interfere, for in this land he was a stranger while Thundercloud was, or could have been, a lord, the old man chose a bed and mattress which, because of their size and weight, were not going to be easy to load on to his barrow. He did not ask for Willie's assistance but Willie gave it just the same. Overloaded and liable to coup over at any minute, the barrow was then pushed by the old man in the direction of his distant home. Willie would not have liked to push it a hundred yards. Joe had to do it for six miles or rather seven because it refused to go in a straight line and kept making divagations.

Willie watched him zig-zag into the desert. Twice the load toppled off and had to be restored. This was done patiently.

'You know,' muttered Willie to the dog, 'I could believe he once led a charge against cavalry.'

There were many Willie Hoggs, most of them ordinary and some not very creditable, but the one there, under that immense pink sky, gazing after the old Indian was one he was proud of, though he would tell no one about him, not even Maggie and certainly not the cynics of the *Airlie Arms*.

The first arrivals came just after eight and stoically took up their positions, squatting on the ground. By half-past nine – Willie kept looking at his watch – more were there than should have been. Bartholomew Simpson, not in the least abashed by his repulse the night before, came to Willie and complained that a family from a distant part of the Reservation, one not covered by the Mission, had turned up, though ineligible. They did not have cards certifying that they were Red Bluffs members. It seemed to Willie a legitimate complaint but when he went to interview and expel the interlopers he found himself confronted by some of the neediest and saddest people he had ever seen. The father was thin and consumptive, the mother scared and woebegone, and the six children ill-nourished and apathetic. How could they, who needed it most, be denied a share? Yet Simpson had logic and justice on his side when he pointed out that if the cards of membership were not to be honoured there could be dozens of outsiders demanding share.

Willie sought advice.

Randy declined to give any.

Maggie disappointed him by saying, sensibly, a rule was a rule.

Elspeth who was in bed reminded him that the people of San Diego had intended their donations solely for members of the Mission.

'I understaun' that,' he said, 'but who's going to tell them? Who's going to send them away?'

'I'm afraid it will have to be you, William.'

Maggie nodded. He felt let down by her.

'Why me? I'm naebody here.'

'I've been watching, Willie,' said Maggie. 'They look up to you.'

Maybe the weans did, he thought ruefully. Most of the men and some of the women were taller than he.

He just could not go to that miserable, unlucky family and send them away, empty-handed. So he took the father aside and slipped fifty dollars of the Fund money into his hand. As he did so he heard in his mind the mocking voice of commonsense: 'Give them money and they'll spend it on hooch.' What would David Hume have said? More to the point what else was Willie Hogg of Glasgow going to do? Like a soldier on parade he marched across to where hundreds of cans of food were stacked, collected a large armful, and took them back to the woman and her children.

No war cries were heard. No tomahawks whizzed through the air. No arrow struck between his shoulders. On the contrary, when he took courage and looked round he saw all those brown eyes gazing at him curiously as if, having just performed one act of magic, he might be about to perform another. Some were even smiling. Suddenly all of them began to shout, not in anger but in acclamation.

Not even Rembrandt could have portrayed Willie's face then.

It would not have been altogether true to say that thereafter the share-out went without a hitch. There were minor disputes, there was one bout of hair-tugging, and there was a prolonged tug-of-war with a handsome big sofa as the rope, but on the whole it went much better than Randy had anticipated and the credit was Willie's. By the end of the day he ached all over and his voice was hoarse, but he was pleased with his day's work. It was a pity he had no grandchildren to tell it to. At the finish, when the last can had been handed over Bartholomew Simpson came up to Willie and hung a necklace round his neck; composed of buffalo teeth, it was learned later. With it was conferred honorary membership of the Chapter: an honour given to few white men.

What pleased him most was Maggie's praise, though, as one Glaswegian to another, it was not expressed extravagantly. 'You did very well, Willie, considering.' He did not have to ask what considering meant. He knew. He grinned. He felt very happy. Why had it taken him so long to admit that he loved and needed her?

16

That night he was in the church playing in the lamplight some Scottish tunes on the piano at Maggie's request. She was in bed, with the door of her room open. He had tucked her in. She had had 'a wee pain' in her left shoulder. Indigestion, she had said. She had asked him to rub it.

He was in the midst of his third rendering of 'Sweet Afton' when he heard a cry. At first he thought it came from outside, but it had come from Maggie. A cry of pain but also of fear and appeal.

He stopped playing. There was a moment's silence, save for his own frightened breathing. Then she cried out again. 'Oh Willie!'

He rushed to her in such a hurry that he banged his knee on the piano. It was to be a painful bruise for weeks but he did not notice it then.

An awful change had come over her. Minutes ago her face had been happy and serene; now it was swollen and distressed. She fought for breath. Through stounds of pain she recognised him. 'Oh Willie, haud me, please haud me.' He held her. 'For Christ's sake, Maggie, don't leave me,' he muttered, but she did not hear him. With a last great shudder she went slack and stopped breathing.

He could not believe it. It was too sudden, too brief, too undeserved. He still held her tight. He kissed her brow, it was already cold. Her mouth fell open. She would have hated looking like that so he gently closed it. When he let go it fell open again. He felt useless, desolate, and unsafe. Inimical forces threatened him.

But he was wasting time. He must go for help. Yet what help was there? He had seen too many deaths not to be sure.

He laid her down gently, closed her mouth again, and limped – why was he limping? – out of the church to Randy's hut.

Randy was as usual reading and listening to music. He looked up in alarm. 'What is it, Willie?'

'It's Maggie. She's gone.'

'Gone?'

'Deid. Just like that.' He snapped his fingers. 'A couple of minutes ago.'

Randy got up. 'Are you sure?'

'Aye. She just said "Oh Willie" and then she died.'

They went together to the church, under stars of great brilliance.

Randy took Maggie's hand, with a vague intention of checking her pulse but he quickly let go. He had tears in his eyes. Why, wondered Willie, have I none in mine?

'Better let Elspeth know,' muttered Randy.

'Aye. You go, Randy. I cannae leave her again.'

'Yes, of course.'

Randy went off, with a haste that wasn't necessary, while Willie sat beside his wife, holding up her chin. There was nothing else he could do for her.

As he waited a curious anger possessed him. It wasn't directed against God or Fate or whatever it was that had ordered this unjust execution and so cruelly and swiftly carried it out. It was directed against himself. He had left so many things undone. That Cross on top of the church for instance. He had promised Elspeth to climb up and straighten it. It would have taken him only a few minutes.

Elspeth came in, wrapped in blankets and wearing mocassins. You're the one who was supposed to die, he thought, and immediately felt chided, by Maggie.

Elspeth knelt by her sister's bed. What was intended as a medical examination became silent prayer.

'I've telephoned for a doctor and ambulance,' said Randy.

'Thanks, Randy.'

It was useless but it had to be done.

'I can't tell you how very sorry I am, Willie. She was a fine lady.'

'So she was.'

'God is merciful,' said Elspeth. 'She did not suffer much.'

She had suffered a great deal but it hadn't lasted long. As for God being merciful, well, you might as well think so, if you believed in Him. There would be little point in believing in a merciless God. And if you didn't believe in Him the question didn't arise. Had Maggie believed in Him? No.

He remembered that he had not yet shed a tear. He would, later, when he was alone. He would weep often. Charlie McCann still wept, after fifty years.

He went forward and pulled a sheet over her face.

'Excuse me,' he said to Elspeth, with great courtesy. Maggie would have wanted him to be very polite to her sister then.

Maggie was still there but not for long. Soon she would be a million miles away.

'I wasnae fair to her,' he said.

It was true but inadequate. He could imagine Maggie shaking her head.

Randy spoke for her. 'Don't reproach yourself, Willie.' But he said it with a bitterness she would never have approved of.

'I'll have to be fair to her noo,' said Willie. 'She always wanted to be buried beside her mither, and her faither. I'll have to take her hame.'

'And she wanted a Christian burial,' said Elspeth. 'She told me that since she was denied a Christian marriage she wanted a Christian burial.'

Willie was dismayed. He did not know whether to believe her or not. Would a Christian, a missionary at that, deliberately and maliciously lie?

'She never complained to me be aboot no' having a Christian marriage. Oors was a guid marriage, as you've admitted yourself. It lasted forty-seven years and it was daith that ended it. How many Christian marriages as you ca' them last as long? We were loyal to each ither though we swore nae oaths to ony ootsider. It was oor business, hers and mine, and naebody else's.'

'God gave you His blessing without you knowing it.'

He could have been offended by that but it wasn't a time for taking offence. He simply said: 'She never said onything to me aboot wanting a Christian burial.'

'She said it to me.'

'What difference does it make?' asked Randy.

That perhaps was the reasonable attitude to take. Who knew what the truth was? But Willie couldn't accept it. He would never be able to endure hearing a minister who had never known Maggie utter a standard eulogy at her graveside. Yet what if that was really what she had wanted? Perhaps she had said it to her sister, without meaning it? Surely if she had meant it she would have said it to him. She had once told him at her mother's grave that she knew she would never see her mother again. 'I'm no' a wean, Willie, to believe that. Talking to her here's my way of remembering her, that's a'.'

'Am I not to be considered?' asked Elspeth. 'If she is buried here in America I could be present.'

If you last that long, thought Willie, for her face looked as deathlike as her sister's under the sheet.

He shook his head. 'I'm sorry. I promised.' Besides he would want to visit the grave every Sunday afternoon.

How, though, to have her taken from this remote place in Arizona to Janefield Cemetery in the heart of Glasgow, thousands of miles away? It would cost a great deal. Well, there was the Fund. There was also, come to think of it, the insurance. He would have to look at the policy.

Sensible wee Willie Hogg, planning the funeral minutes after the death. He needed Maggie's advice.

He had begun to tremble. He was losing control of himself.

'Are you all right, Willie?' asked Randy.

'Would it be keeping my promise if I had her cremated here and took her ashes to scatter them on her mother's grave?' Her father's grave too. Poor David McCrae was still being forgotten.

'I think it would, near enough,' said Randy, 'but I don't think Maggie would.'

'No, she wouldn't.'

'Am I to have no say?' asked Elspeth. 'She was my sister.'

They heard the ambulance arrive then, with a scattering of stones.

There was a young doctor with it. It took him a couple of minutes to confirm that Maggie was dead, of a heart attack. These things happened, his manner implied. She was an old woman. It was a pity but not a surprise. He was more concerned about Elspeth.

'How are you yourself, Mrs Hansen? Changed your mind about going into hospital?'

She took them all aback by replying, 'Yes, doctor.'

Willie and Randy exchanged astonished glances.

'Do you want me to make the arrangements?' asked the doctor.

Randy intervened. 'They are already made. They will send a plane from San Diego.'

'Good. The sooner the better. If I can be of any help please call on me.' With hardly a change of tone he added: 'Do you want us to remove the deceased?'

Willie shook his head. 'I'll look after her tonight.'

He felt foolishly resentful at how little help the doctor and ambulance men had been. He would have to be careful. He couldn't go about blaming people. Maggie would have been the first to rebuke him.

When at last they were all gone and he was alone in the church, save for Maggie, he sat down again at the piano and played over and over again 'Sweet Afton'. Outside the old dog howled mournfully, as if it knew.

When he stopped and there was silence in the church except for a mouse-like scraping in a corner, he murmured, 'Dear, dear Maggie', and shed tears.

17

Charlie McCann had once told how *he* had tried to cope with his wife's unexpected and early death. He had pretended that she was not gone for good but only for a limited period, three months say, visiting her family in North Ireland and in time she would come back. In that way her presence could at first be with him, at his work as he swept the streets, in his house as he cooked himself a meal or washed the dishes or nursed his cat. His hope had been that as the wound of his loss grew less painful he would be able to accept that he would never see or hear or touch her again, but it hadn't worked out like that. After fifty years he still missed her: the wound had never healed.

Unlike Charlie, Willie had urgent things to do, on Maggie's behalf. Attending to them postponed grief.

Next morning, as soon as it was light enough to read by, he got out the insurance policy and quickly found the relevant passage, printed in pale blue characters. 'The Insurer will pay up to £1,000,000 for each insured person in respect of the transfer of the Insured person's body or ashes in the event of death to the United Kingdom (excluding funeral and interment expenses.)'

He heard a voice in his mind: 'Am I to be sent hame like a parcel?'

'I'll be on the same plane, hen.'

He could not ask her if it was true that she had told Elspeth she wanted a minister at her burial.

Well, he could and did but she, under the sheet, could not and did not answer.

After breakfast he took the insurance policy to let Randy see it. It was a solitary meal. Elspeth felt too ill to eat and the three old women remained in their room, mourning Maggie. Their crooning, with occasional wails, froze his blood.

'It certainly looks as if you're fully covered,' said Randy.

'So what do I do? I expect there are undertakers in Holbrook.'

'They call themselves morticians here. I suppose any competent practitioner could arrange it all.'

'As far as Prestwick.'

'It would seem so.'

'A Glasgow undertaker would take over then.'

There was one in his district: Mr Chalmers. He looked more like a bookie with his fancy waistcoats but was said to be efficient and not too expensive.

'Is there anyone you should inform, Willie? Any close relative of yours or Maggie's?'

'No. We were on oor ain.'

'Friends, maybe?'

'Weel yes, we have freends.' But not, he now realised, anyone very close. It was a discovery that shook him. He had known that he was a private little bugger but not as private as that. Not even Charlie could be called an intimate friend.

'Maybe I should send a notice to the *Glasgow Herald*. That's the paper where death notices are published.'

'Yes, you could do that. What about the newspaper that published the article about you?'

'I think I'd rather keep them oot o' it.'

'I understand. Well, shall we pay a visit to Holbrook?'

On the way Willie was tempted to ask Randy if he thought Elspeth was telling the truth when she said that Maggie had expressed a wish to have a Christian burial. He decided it would be unfair. In a very short time Randy would be in the same bleak position as himself. In any case even if your wife was in the best of health you shouldn't be asked if you thought she was a liar.

They drove to the motel to ask the manager if he could recommend a mortician. At first he assumed it was Mrs Hansen who had died for her illness had been known in the town. He was shocked to learn that it was 'the cute little Scotch lady with the hat'.

He recommended Mr Gus Bellingham and warned them not to be put off by that gentleman's unusual garb. Gus had wanted to be a rancher, not a mortician like his father and grandfather before him. But he was a man of initiative who knew his business and could arrange a burial on the moon, if sufficient funds were available.

Well, thought Willie, a few minutes later when he was shaking hands with Mr Bellingham in that gentleman's establishment that smelled of costly wood, would Maggie have disapproved of having her remains being looked after by a man of fifty or so with a moustache like that, a belt like that adorned with little silver figures of cowboys on horseback, a shirt like that, black with glittering sequins, tight fawn breeches like those, and leather boots with heels as high as those? Yes, she would, for she would have liked his soft warm voice and his brown eyes that looked honestly into yours.

She would have appreciated too the enthusiasm with which he undertook the project. He had never done anything so ambitious before, involving an Atlantic crossing, but he was confident he could do it to Mr Hogg's satisfaction, and also to Mrs Hogg's though he did not say so. If Mr Hogg could give him the name of a Glasgow mortician Mr Bellingham would be glad to liaise with him, so that the casket could be met at Prestwick for removal to Glasgow. As for expense, since the insurance company would be paying, there would be no mean little economies but no ostentatious extravagances either. Though he didn't want to, Willie was invited to go into the storeroom full of caskets to take his pick. There was one he thought Maggie would have liked, because of its white satin lining. He chose that one.

It was arranged that Mr Bellingham personally, with an assistant, would go out to the Mission soon after sundown and remove Mrs Hogg to their premises in Holbrook. Everything would then be attended to: death certificates, customs formalities, airline reservations, etc. All that Mr Hogg would have to do was wait and mourn: the hardest lot of all. By this time Mr Hogg's hand was sore from having been shaken so often so firmly. His heart too was numb. Still, he felt grateful.

Afterwards Randy and he went for lunch.

He was worried about being fair to Elspeth. As Maggie's sister she had a right to be present at the funeral.

'Would she want to be buried in Janefield too, with her family?'

'I am her family, Willie.'

'Aye, that's right. I'm sorry. If she wanted to go to Maggie's funeral I'd pay her expenses. Yours too, Randy.'

'We both know she couldn't stand the journey. In any case her church in San Diego will want to bury her. There might even be a bishop present.'

Willie noticed the bitterness. Would he himself feel bitter if there was a minister at Maggie's funeral? Not bitter, no. The man would be trying to help, even if he did haver about everlasting bliss without really believing in it himself. But Willie would feel guilty and ashamed, in that, in the service of the person he had loved most in the world, he had stood by in craven silence while statements were made as facts which he considered at best as hopeful guesses. It would not be his last leave-taking of Maggie; his own death would be that; but it would be a very important stage in their relationship and he would not wish to take part in it acting a lie.

Of course it would make a difference if Maggie had wanted a minister to be present. He would have to respect that. But how to make sure?

18

That afternoon he was in the church, keeping Maggie company, when Randy came to tell him that he was wanted on the telephone.

'Is it Mr Bellingham?' he asked.

'No, Willie. It's from Glasgow.'

'Glasgow?' Willie almost broke down. Maggie's city. The Art Galleries. Kelvingrove Park. Sauchiehall Street.

'Did they say who they were?'

'It's that newspaper, Willie. Somebody called Meiklejohn.'

Willie remembered the cheerful red-haired young reporter. 'Whit did he want?'

'To talk to you.'

'Did you tell him onything?'

'No. I just said I'd fetch you.'

'Thanks, Randy.'

Willie wanted to be allowed to bury his wife in peace and privacy but he could not resist this voice from Glasgow wanting to talk to him.

Canny Glaswegian that he was, he hurried across to the house. That telephone call must be costing another Glaswegian a small fortune.

His hand shook as he lifted the telephone. So did his voice. 'Hello. Willie Hogg here.'

Meiklejohn's voice was so cheerful and so Scottish that tears came into Willie's eyes. I should put this thing doon, he thought, before I start greeting like a wean.

'Hello, Willie, it's nice to hear your voice again. I see you haven't picked up a Yankee accent yet.'

'What do you want, Mr Meiklejohn?'

'Come on, Willie. I'm a reporter following up a story. What's it like at the mission? Bells ringing? Nuns praying? That kind of thing.?'

'No, no.'

'How's your sister-in-law?'

'She's going into hospital in a day or two.'

'So she's had to give in at last?'

'You could say that.'

'How's your wife, Maggie? We all took to Maggie, you know.'

Willie could scarcely speak. 'She's deid. Maggie's deid.'

There was a pause. 'Did I hear right, Willie? Did you say deid?'

'Aye. A heart attack.'

'Jesus Christ! When did it happen?'

'Last night.'

'Willie, I can't say how sorry I am. What a fucking shame, if you'll excuse me putting it like that.'

Aye, Mr Meiklejohn, I'll excuse you. A fucking shame. What was it Willie had read in a poem once? "We are at the mercy of senseless events." That was another way of putting it.

'What are you going to do, Willie? Are you going to bring her home?'

'Aye, She always wanted to be buried in Janefield beside her mither and faither.'

'So she would. When is that likely to be?'

'I don't ken yet, but I would like her funeral to be private.'

'Willie, I can understand you wanting it to be private, and so it will be private, private to Glasgow. It will be nobody's business but Glasgow's. I'm sure she would have wanted that, Willie. She was a true Glaswegian. Who's handling things for you at that end?'

'A Mr Gus Bellingham of Holbrook.'

'Bellingham? Right. Look, Willie. I'll be in touch with you again, very soon. Don't worry about expenses. We'll take care of those. In the meantime, Willie, remember this: you've got the whole city behind you.'

But, thought Willie, as he put the telephone down, I'm not sure I want the whole city behind me.

In the living-room Randy was looking out of the window. 'Look at this, Willie.'

Willie looked and was amazed to see, gathered in front of the church, where Maggie lay, a large company of Indians, men and women. They were performing a solemn and stately dance and chanting a song of mourning.

The old dog was joining in, with a prolonged howl.

Among the Indians were Elspeth's three lodgers.

'Should I go and thank them?' asked Willie.

'No need. It's a tribute to both you and Maggie.'

'She would have appreciated it.'

Two or three minutes later they were gone, as unobtrusively as they had come.

Willie noticed that the three old women had gone with them.

The dog looked more bewildered than ever.

'Who was it on the telephone, Willie?'

'The reporter, Mr Meiklejohn.'

'He wouldn't know?'

'No. He was quite upset. He said they'd a' taken to her. I told him I wanted the funeral to be private. He said so it would be. Private to Glasgow, he said. I'm no' sure whit he meant exactly.'

'I think what he meant, Willie, was that a lot of Glasgow people would want to be present.'

'But I said in the notice to the *Herald* that it was to be private.'

'Still, lots of people will want to be there.'

'Aye, likely enough.'

'In a way, Willie, in an honourable way, the Fund made you and Maggie public property.'

'But I never wanted that. I've a guid mind to cancel the whole thing and have her buried here.' But he didn't really mean it. His promise had to be kept and he wasn't at all sure that Maggie wouldn't have been pleased to have lots of Glasgow folk watching her being united with her mother.

'You wouldn't do that, Willie.'

'No.'

It was then sundown. Not long afterwards Mr Bellingham arrived with an assistant and a hearse. Willie went over to the church. It might be his last chance to look at Maggie, but he found when he got there that he didn't want to look and so he kept out of the way and let the undertakers get on with their work. This they did deftly and reverently, though they were wearing cowboy hats, black in colour.

Before he left Mr Bellingham came to Willie and gave him a little red box. 'Her wedding-ring, Mr Hogg. I thought you would like to have it.'

'Thanks.'

'If you'd like to call in tomorrow I'd be able to give you some idea of how the arrangements are getting on. I should point out it would be your last chance of looking upon your loved one.'

'Thanks.'

'Another thing. I've had a call from a newspaper reporter in Glasgow, a Mr Meiklejohn. He said you knew him. He wanted me to give him some information regarding the arrangements. I told him I would have to consult you. If he asks again should I give him the information he wants? I should say he could probably find it out from other sources.'

Well, at least Meiklejohn wouldn't have a piper playing laments at Prestwick airport. Or would he? How far did reporters go nowadays to build up a story? Meiklejohn had said he would telephone Willie again. He could be reminded then to consider Willie's feelings.

'Tell him to phone me, Mr Bellingham. I'll discuss it with him.'

'Excellent. In the meantime I hope to see you tomorrow, about three o'clock, shall we say?'

'I'll be there.'

Maggie would be there too.

About half an hour after the undertakers had left Meiklejohn telephoned. His voice was subdued. 'Well, Willie, how are you?'

'Bearing up.' He could not resist adding, proudly, 'The Indians have just been to do a dance in front of the church in honour of Maggie.'

'I'd have liked to see that, Willie. There's going to be a piece in the paper tomorrow but don't worry, you wouldn't find it offensive. I wrote it myself and I kept thinking of Maggie as if she was my own mother. You're not alone, Willie. All Glasgow's with you. When do you expect to get back? You'll be flying to Prestwick?'

'Aye, but I don't ken when. It's no' fixed yet. Mr Meiklejohn, I don't want my wife's funeral turned into a kind of circus.'

'Neither do I, Willie. It won't be, I assure you.'

'There'll be naebody there selling toffee aipples?'

It took Meiklejohn about five seconds to realise that was a joke and a brave Glaswegian one at that. 'Not even hot pies, Willie.'

It occurred to Willie then that it might be wet and cold on the day of the funeral. He hoped not, though it would reduce the number of sightseers.

'Well, Willie, see you soon. Once again, my sincerest sympathy.'

'Thanks.'

Willie put down the telephone and then realised he had nowhere to go and never would have. Where Maggie was had been home for him. She was everywhere now but he felt utterly homeless and would go on being so for the rest of his life.

Randy was sitting with Elspeth.

Willie looked in. He gasped at how yellow and shrivelled her face had become during the past two days. So she's had to give in, Meiklejohn had said. She hadn't, for there she was smiling at him, but defeat, if not surrender, was now in sight. She would not see it as defeat, though; especially if she was to be ushered into the Lord's presence by a bishop. Don't be bitter, he told himself. Don't be mean.

'I'm going oot for a wee walk,' he said.

'Where to?' asked Randy, in some alarm.

'Just roundaboot.'

'You'd better take a torch.'

'The stars are bricht enough.'

'It's easy to get lost out there, Willie. Don't go far. Keep an eye on the light in the window.'

'I'll dae that.' Willie smiled at Elspeth.

As soon as he came out of the house the dog crept up to him, whimpering. Though he remembered the scabs on its head he patted it. Poor beast, he thought, in a day or two this place will be deserted. What will you do then? Maybe I could bribe one of the Indians to take you in and look after you. But could he be trusted? Here I am, worrying about an old scabby mongrel when Maggie's lying dead in the undertaker's parlour in Holbrook and all over the world millions are hungry. I should kick the bloody thing in the teeth or do it a greater kindness still by smashing in its head with a large stone. That would teach it to trust nobody. But wasn't that a lesson it had learned long ago?

He stopped and held up both clenched fists to the stars.

At his feet the dog whined. It wasn't blaming him. It had long since given up blaming anyone.

He turned. Yonder was the light in the window. It represented home of a kind. He began to walk back towards it.

The dog followed.

He would open a can of meat and give the poor brute a feast.

He heard a voice. 'It's no' really a kindness to feed it, Willie. It'll just become attached to you and when you go it'll break its hert.'

True, Maggie, but I'm going to feed it just the same.

20

Next day an ambulance came to take Elspeth to the airport. It was accompanied by a taxi containing a doctor from the hospital in San Diego and an official of Elspeth's church in that city. They had flown up in a private plane and were taking her back in it. When it was far too late they were stirring themselves. But perhaps, thought Willie, that was unfair. Elspeth had minimised her illness and spurned all offers of help.

The doctor was a young man with longish hair. He did not talk as if he was religious himself. He chatted with Willie in the sunshine. The dog sat at Willie's feet.

'Well, doctor, how is she?'

'Very poorly, I'm afraid.'

'She's not got much chance of recovery, has she?'

'Not unless there's a miracle and it'd have to be bloody quick.' He looked all round him. 'I once heard a leader of the Apostolic Church say how generous we had been to these poor benighted heathens: a thousand acres per family. A thousand acres of stony nothing. I would think faith would have as hard a time flourishing here as wheat.'

Willie wasn't so sure. When the Indians had paid tribute to Maggie it had been a kind of faith, if not in God then in humanity, and even as he and the doctor were talking trucks and cars were arriving with Indians come to see Elspeth leave.

'It depends on whit you mean by faith,' he said.

The doctor then remembered that he was speaking to a relative of Mrs Hansen's, someone too whose wife had died in this godforsaken place a day or so ago, and who belonged to a nation famed or rather notorious for its obsession with religion.

He did not reply to Willie's cautious remark. Instead he studied the Indians. 'Strange people,' he muttered. 'This could be the moon and they its inhabitants. I understand tuberculosis is rife among them.'

'Excuse me a minute, doctor,' said Willie. 'I want to talk to them.'

He walked over to the Indians. It was curious, there were no women among them this time.

The dog followed.

He approached Bartholomew Simpson. 'Hello, Mr Simpson,' he said.

Simpson eyed him solemnly.

'I expect you've heard that Mrs Hansen is leaving this morning. She is being taken to hospital in San Diego.'

'Will she come back?'

'No. She is going to die soon.'

They looked down on women as inferior. They would not let women eat with them. What place would they think was there in the Happy Hunting Grounds for a woman, white at that, who had dared to assume authority over them? Were they congratulating themselves that she would be given some menial task like the cleaning out of privies?

'Would you like to see her before she leaves?' he asked.

They did not even shake their heads. They just stood and stared.

'Weel, I'll tell her you came.'

Suddenly, to his consternation, for he had wanted to look manly, tears came into his eyes. He was remembering Maggie.

They must despise him, this small white man with the woman's tears, but he did not care.

The dog growled, as if it thought he needed its protection.

'This poor beast,' he said. 'It's going to be left on its ain.'

They stared at it: a miserable creature, not worth eating, so their eyes said.

'As you can see it's affectionate. Perhaps one of you with children could take it. I'll give twenty dollars to anyone willing to look after it.'

He did not feel virtuous as he said that; he felt foolish. They looked at him as if they thought he was a fool.

None took up his offer. Perhaps it wasn't enough.

'I'll make it fifty dollars.' The Fund would pay.

Their stares were not quite so stolid then. Fifty dollars would keep a family for a month. The dog, if it was lucky, might get a bone thrown at it. When the money was done it would be driven off.

He had the fifty dollars in his hand.

A young man stepped forward and took the money. From his pocket he took a piece of string and tied it round the dog's neck. It growled and showed its teeth but calmed down when Willie spoke to it.

'Treat it well,' he said, and added, foolishly, 'For the Great Spirit's sake.'

Then he walked back towards the house. The dog whined and tried to follow him.

They were ready to carry Elspeth out to the ambulance.

The church official had white hair and a dark suit. He spoke to Willie. 'Excuse me, are you Mr Hogg?'

'That's right.'

'Mrs Hansen would like to speak to you in private.'

Willie nodded. He had intended to go in and say goodbye.

'Don't keep her long, Mr Hogg.'

'I won't. Tell me, whit's going to happen to this place? Will it be abandoned?'

'Probably.'

'No one willing to tak' it on?'

'It has not been a rewarding post. By the way, Mr Hogg, I was very sorry to hear about your wife. It must be a comfort to know that she is with the Lord. I have heard her spoken of as a good woman.'

'Aye. Do you ken where Mr Hansen is?'

'He is with Mrs Hansen.' He could not keep censure out of his voice, God knew what he blamed poor Randy for. The failure of the Mission was the least of it.

Willie went into the house. Randy was in the bedroom with Elspeth.

'You wanted to see me, Elspeth?'

'Yes, William.' Her voice was weak but still determined.

'Would you like me to leave?' asked Randy.

'No, Randolph, I want you here as a witness.'

Randy and Willie looked at each other.

'I was not telling the truth when I said Margaret wanted a Christian burial.'

Willie did not feel triumphant. 'Weel, thanks for telling me.'

'She said "Willie and me don't believe in that kind of thing. When I die Willie will speak at my grave." I always thought, William, that being a simple soul, she was under your influence.'

'She had a mind of her ain.'

'I see that now. I did not want to die with a lie on my conscience. I hope you do give her a Christian burial. Goodbye, William.'

He went forward and, surprising himself and her too, did not merely take her hand but bent down and kissed her on the brow. It had many things in it, that kiss. Forgiveness was one.

'Goodbye, Elspeth.'

'You always tried to be a good man, William Hogg.'

He blinked at that.

Then in came the ambulance men to carry her out.

Randy was going with Elspeth in the plane. It meant that in a minute or two Willie would be left alone on the mission.

He and Randy shook hands.

'You might want to come to San Diego one day, Willie. I'd be very glad to see you.'

'And you might want to come to Glasgow.'

'I might at that. Mr Bellingham will send a car for you, Willie. You'll be spending the night in Holbrook. Certainly not here.' Randy looked about him and shuddered.

'I'm wondering what to dae aboot Maggie's things. No' that she had sich a lot.'

'Just leave them in the house, Willie. Some woman will pick them up. Maggie would have liked that.'

'So she would.'

'Good luck anyway. Be sure and write.'

'You too.'

He watched the ambulance and the taxi drive off in clouds of shining stour.

The Indians were gone too, taking the dog with them.

Ought he, before the car came for him, to straighten that bloody Cross?

Part Three

1

Often during the long flight home, economy class this time, Willie thought of Maggie and how empty his life was going to be without her. Once he found himself wishing that the plane would be blown up by a bomb. Then, looking at the passengers near him, one a little girl of about eight, he was horrified by his monstrous self-pity. He wanted that little girl to grow up to be a happy woman with children of her own. He wanted everyone on the plane, everyone in the whole world, to stay alive and be happy.

He wondered at times if the stewardesses knew who he was, or rather knew that he was the passenger with the peculiar luggage in the hold, for it seemed to him that though they smiled with professional charm at all the passengers their smiles for him had a special quality of compassion. But then everyone's smile for him seemed to have that quality. Even the old woman behind him in the queue for the toilet whose fidgetting indicated, as it was meant to, that her need was more urgent than his: so that he had to let her go before him.

None of them knew about Maggie and therefore this special quality in their smiles was imagined by him, but all the same he was sure that if they had known they would have smiled at him in that way; even those poor souls terrified of flying.

He felt at times that the destiny of the human race – no, that was daft – well, the good name of the human race was in his keeping. That was daft too but still he felt it. What had happened to him, the loss of a person he had loved dearly, happened to most human beings at one time or another. It had to be tholed with courage and dignity and without resentment. He must wish everyone well and no one ill. He must do it for humanity's sake and not for God's.

He was so engrossed in these thoughts that he was slow to become aware that the woman beside him wanted to go to the toilet again: this was her third time. She was fat too and had difficulty getting in and out of her seat. She was looking at him with reproach. Evidently this was not the first time she had asked him to excuse her. When he apologised and quickly got up to let her pass she smiled in forgiveness and understanding. He was old and probably deaf. He wasn't as quick on the uptake as he once had been. Since he was travelling by himself his wife either was dead or he had never been married. Poor old fellow.

He had been assured by Mr Bellingham that representatives of the Glasgow undertaker would be at Prestwick to meet the plane, even though its time of landing was 7.15 am. That had been too early for Mr Meiklejohn. He had telephoned Willie at the motel. 'I'll drop in and see you at your house, Willie, once you've recovered from the journey. Take a taxi from Prestwick. Charge it to us.'

Willie had also been told that an official of the airport would meet him and help him through the formalities. There was a conspiracy of kindness to make things as easy for him as possible.

So it happened. As the passengers streamed through the door into the arrivals' lounge there was a man in uniform holding a card with MR HOGG written on it. 'That's me,' said Willie, and while the other passengers looked on in surmise, wondering if he was a drugs smuggler or escaped criminal, he was led past passport control and customs and along unending corridors.

The official made polite conversation. 'I would have recognised you from your picture in the newspaper, Mr Hogg.'

'Oh.'

'May I offer you my sympathy? My wife's too. Would you believe it when I tell you she burst into tears when she read about your wife? She wouldn't be the only one in Glasgow, I can tell you.'

'She must have a guid hert, your wife.'

'Did you have a good flight?'

He asked out of habit. He saw at once his mistake and looked ashamed. But Willie smiled and said he had.

The rest of the world, he knew, had their own concerns and woes. He couldn't expect them to be thinking about his all the time. That was the last thing he wanted.

He hoped that Mr Chalmers hadn't sent a hearse for the coffin or casket as Mr Bellingham had called it. So he was relieved to find a plain black van waiting for him. The driver, a tall thin man with black sideburns, was standing by it smoking a cigarette. He hurriedly put it out as Willie approached but Willie was pleased to see him smoking, though it was at all other times a dirty, deleterious habit which he himself had given up years ago. Here it was a sign of human complicity.

The driver gave his name as Eddie Jeffrey. Willie suspected that, in his uniform, driving a hearse or a black Rolls Royce he would call himself Edward. He explained that Mr Chalmers had not been able to come in person: he had other business to see to that morning. He sent his apologies and was sure Mr Hogg would understand. Mr Hogg did. Other men's wives died too.

Willie was taken to where he had to sign some papers, and then to the carousel for his suitcase. It was the only one left on it.

In front of the airport buildings he saw some seagulls. His grief then was at its sharpest. The birds represented what Maggie had lost. He remembered her feeding them on the steamer to Rothesay long ago.

He was considering whether to hire a taxi to take him to Glasgow – the *Daily Chronicle* would pay – when the van reappeared. Eddie got out. He said he had not liked in the circumstances to ask Mr Hogg if he wanted a lift to Glasgow, but it was not convenient by bus or train, especially as it was raining and still dark, and a taxi would be very expensive. Willie gladly accepted. He had travelled with Maggie in the plane, he would travel with her in the van too.

The driver found a place for the suitcase in the van. Willie took care not to glance in.

With Willie seated beside him the driver drove off. As might be expected of a man in his trade he wasn't talkative.

Willie spoke twice during the journey.

Looking out at the wet streets of Glasgow he said: 'It's guid to be hame' and 'I'd be obliged, Mr Jeffrey, if you'd drap me ootside my close, I'll tell you when we come to it.'

They arrived at the close-mouth about a quarter to ten. Luckily there were few people about and they cowered under umbrellas.

Nobody paid any attention to the black van. It could have been delivering a three-piece suite.

'If you'd like to go up and let yourself in, Mr Hogg,' said Eddy, 'I'll bring up your case.' He had noticed that Willie was anxious not to be seen.

So Willie, with his cap drawn down over his eyes, sneaked out of the van and up the stairs. He met no one. The key rattled in the lock, so shaky was his hand. The door opened and he stepped in, on to letters scattered on the floor.

Eddy followed with the case. He put it down in the living-room. He looked about him and saw the photograph on the mantelpiece of Willie and Maggie and the swans, but was too good at his job to remark upon it.

'See you on Wednesday then, Mr Hogg.'

Today was Monday. The funeral was to be on Wednesday.

'Aye, sure. Thanks very much, Mr Jeffrey. You've been very kind.'

The driver then broke one of his rules: don't offer sympathy to the bereaved, however much he felt it. Like a doctor or nurse he had to put on an appearance of professional competence, that was all. People preferred that.

But this was different. Here was a lonely, confused old man who had come thousands of miles with his dead wife to an empty house.

'Will you be all right, Mr Hogg?'

'Aye, aye. I'll be a' right.'

But when the driver was gone Willie sat on a chair in the once familiar and homely house that would never be familiar and homely again, and wept.

2

After a while he made himself tea. It took him some time for he had trouble in remembering where things were. He had to do it all quietly so as not to let his neighbours through the wall know that he was back. He felt mean about this but wasn't ready yet to face their condolences, genuine and heart-warming though these would be. Everything was strange: the kettle, the teapot, and the cup decorated with red not yellow flowers. It was as if he had come from another planet and had been away for years, instead of only 12 days. It would have been shorter too if he hadn't had to hang about Holbrook while Mr Bellingham sorted out some entanglements and, as he'd delicately hinted, done a little necessary embalming.

He liked milk in his tea but had to do without. He kept looking at the letters which he had picked up and placed on the table. There were twenty-three. Who had sent them? Maggie and he had gone months, no years, without receiving so many. It must be because of the article in the newspaper. He noticed they were addressed to him c/o the *Daily Chronicle*. Two of the envelopes were black-edged. Should he read them all or just dump them in the bin under the sink? Was there a bin under the sink? Was it blue or red? If he read them should he answer them? What would Maggie have said? 'It's only good manners to answer letters, Willie.'

He felt very tired but did not want to lie down. He would never have been able to sleep. Memories would have haunted him.

All the time he had a great fear that if he did not hold on tightly he would slip down into imbecility and end up in hospital like poor Jack.

Perhaps these letters would help him to hold on. They must have been written by well-wishers interested in him. That surely was what he needed most now, the encouragement of his fellow man.

It turned out though that almost all of them had been sent by women. He picked one up at random. The notepaper, like the envelope, was mauve and scented. The handwriting was small, neat, and assertive. It was from a woman who signed herself Martha Naismith. She was a widow. Her husband had died six months ago of cancer of the lungs: he had been a heavy smoker. She still missed him, especially in bed. (There were six exclamation marks after that.) She was only sixty-three, still in her prime. Given the chance, she could help Mr Hogg to get over his loss and he could help her to get over hers. Being a member of the Church of Scotland she would like to talk to him about his visit to the Mission. If he replied she would enclose a photograph with her next letter. In a postscript she mentioned that she had a three-bedroomed bungalow in Riddrie.

He did not dare imagine Maggie's comments.

He opened others. It was more or less the same story in every one. They were from lonely, unhappy women, desperate for companionship. One or two, not so innocent, hinted at the large amount of money he had got from the newspaper and the Fund. They would be delighted to help him spend it in having a good time, in some warm sunny place like the South of Spain. One enclosed a colour photograph. It showed a bold woman of about fifty-five – she didn't give her age – with hair that looked dyed, big bosom, and rouged cheeks. She had had four children – now grown-up – so she knew what was what, if he saw what she meant. She was sure that she and Mr Hogg – may I call you Willie? – could make sweet music together. He had never liked the phrase. Here he found it disgusting.

One letter was a relief, although it was obviously fraudulent. It was from a man, a Mr Tom Hanlon, who wrote that he had bad lungs, had been out of work for three years, had lost his wife a year ago, and had three little girls, one mentally retarded. Given a helping hand, he could overcome all these troubles. If Mr Hogg could see fit to send him a modest sum, a hundred pounds say, he would receive the gratitude of an unhappy father and three sad wee girls. Even five pounds would do.

Well Maggie, what should I say to Mr Hanlon?

Maybe, Willie, he *has* a wee lassie that's backward.

And bad lungs?

There are lots of unfortunate folk in the world.

Should I gie him money then?

That's up to you, Willie. I'm out of the game.

Yes, Maggie, love, you are out of the game.

On only one envelope was the address typewritten. It had been sent direct to the house. It was from Councillor Spence in his capacity as chairman of the William Hogg Travel Fund committee. He conveyed the committee's sympathy and then went on to enquire about the Fund. How much had been spent, how much remained, and were receipts available? He apologised for bringing up such matters at such a time but he knew that Mr Hogg as an honest and responsible man would understand.

Yes, and Mr Hogg would greatly enjoy seeing the councillor's face when he saw the receipt from the Excelsior hotel in Phoenix.

What Mr Hogg needed was a refuge, not only from mercenary and passionate widows, crass councillors, and predatory reporters but also from himself. He might find it, as he had done before, in the Art Galleries.

3

He wasn't content, like most visitors, to promenade from one large room to another, giving every picture, whatever its size or subject, and whoever the artist, the same five seconds of attention. He would sit for half an hour at a stretch on one of the hard wooden benches in front of a painting likely, in his present state of mind, to give him inspiration and comfort. One of these should have been Salvador Dali's "Crucifixion". In spite of its reputation Willie had always been uneasy about it. It was too slick for his taste, more concerned with pictorial effect than with humanity. Today he found far less reassurance in it than he had done in the robin he had seen in a bush at the entrance to the Galleries. By its very ordinariness the little bird had seemed to him to hold the world together more effectively than this brilliant but showy picture.

When the Glasgow Corporation had bought it for what had then been considered an exorbitant price there had been an outcry against municipal extravagance, but admission money had been charged to see it and soon the city had got its money back, with a handsome profit thrown in. Today it could be seen for nothing. Perhaps, thought Willie, in these days of money-worship, it would have had more to say to him if he had had to pay to see it.

He was ashamed of himself for that cynical reflection. He bade himself remember the generosity shown him by many strangers.

As a humanist he had always regretted that the great artists of the Italian Renaissance, like Titian and Raphael, had expended so much of their time and talent in trying to portray divinity, surely an impossible quest, with the result that their treatment of Christian themes, such as the Madonna and Child, was so often stilted and insipid.

It had always been a mystery to him that Christ's death on the Cross should have come to be regarded as the central pillar of the Christian faith: since, it was believed, he had died to save mankind. Apart from the fact that mankind, in an age of nuclear bombs was in danger of annihilation, was it not the case that since then millions, many millions, of ordinary men and women, not to mention children, had suffered more horrible deaths than His?

Today, when he would dearly have loved to be able to believe and so be assured that he would one day see Maggie again, he made an effort to banish from his mind all doubts and prejudices, as he went from one religious painting to another, hoping for a sign that would set his soul on fire, just as he had hoped for one during the service conducted by Elspeth in the church at Red Bluffs. I want to be convinced and uplifted, he said to those paintings. Convince me, please. Uplift me.

He rebuked himself, he mocked himself, an ex-hospital porter who had left school at fourteen with no certificates, who as a soldier had been more useful at cleaning out latrines than killing the enemy, and who lived in a council flat on two meagre pensions, daring to find inadequate and unsatisfying a religion that had lasted almost two thousand years, had had a multitude of books written about it by men much wiser and more knowledgable than he, and had had magnificent cathedrals built in its honour.

Nonetheless he was still not convinced or uplifted.

Meanwhile the attendants, who were on special alert after a painting worth millions had been slashed by a madman in London, had begun to eye suspiciously the old fellow with the cloth cap. Was he, God forbid, a rabid Orangeman, getting ready to destroy one of these Catholic paintings? Did he have a knife or hatchet concealed in his raincoat pocket? They noticed how he would sit for as long as half an hour staring at a picture. It could be of course that he was not studying it at all but was in a kind of coma. With that face he could hardly be an art connoisseur. He wasn't a tramp, though, come in to shelter from the cold and wet. There was no stink off him. His clothes were plebeian but respectable. His shoes were polished. It wouldn't be easy to find a good reason for ordering him out.

It was noticed at one point that he had tears in his eyes. At the time he seemed to be looking at a self-portrait of Rembrandt in old age.

What he was really looking at was that imaginary masterpiece by William Hogg, of tea being taken in Elspeth's room in the Mission at Red Bluffs.

An attendant, moved more by curiosity than suspicion, went up to him quietly.

'Is there anything wrong, sir' he asked.

'Why should there be onything wrang?'

'You seem disturbed.'

'Weel, aren't these pictures meant to disturb us?'

What could the attendant say to that? That he saw these pictures every day and they never disturbed him?

'You see, my wife dee'd six days ago. In the Arizona desert. On a Christian Mission. On an Navajo reservation. I brought her remains hame this morning in an aeroplane.'

The attendant was nonplussed. Not being a reader of the *Daily Chronicle* he had never heard of Willie Hogg. He was sure he was talking to a lunatic.

He was strengthened in this belief when the old man took from his pocket a woman's necklace of blue beads, saying, 'The Indians gave her this.'

It was some film he had seen on television. Being senile, he had got it mixed up with reality. Probably he had bought the necklace at the Barrows.

'Before I left I straightened the Cross on the church.'

The attendant stared after him. Religious dementia. That must be it. The poor old fellow thought he could perform miracles.

4

He walked home in the rain. On the way he went into a small dingy cafe for a cup of tea and a sausage roll. He sat in a corner, stirring his tea so long that it must have been cold before he drank it; so the woman behind the counter, watching him with pity, was to tell her husband that night. He just nibbled at his sausage roll. He looked as if there was nothing in the world he would enjoy. 'I think his wife must have died recently. He looked lost.'

He felt lost. Yet he had been born and bred in this city. He knew its ways. He spoke its language. Its inhabitants were famed for their helpfulness, but no one even here could give him the directions he needed.

He went into a supermarket outside his district where he wasn't known. He wanted to buy bread, milk, and margarine for his breakfast tomorrow. He'd often done the shopping when Maggie was in a withdrawn mood, so he had that advantage over other elderly widowers who had left it all to their wives. What he would have to be careful about was this feeling of being lost and of giving the appearance of being lost – he had noticed the woman's pity in the cafe – for it could easily become a habit and he'd become known as a pitiful helpless old man. Indeed it happened in the supermarket. The girl at the check-out counter was young and very patient with the old gentleman who couldn't open the plastic bag to put his purchases in; she had to do it for him.

There would be many like her, eager to help; but he must take care not to fall into a condition where he depended too much on other people. Fortunately he had friends who would not allow him to mope in self-pity. He would meet them tomorrow in the *Airlie Arms*. Perhaps it wasn't right for a man whose wife wasn't yet buried to consort with pals in a pub but he would drink only half a pint and their concern for him and their remembrance of Maggie would make it sacramental.

It was still raining and growing dark when he reached his close. He might be lucky enough to get home again without being accosted. After the funeral he would have an open door for his neighbours, but tonight he wanted to be alone.

As luck would have it, outside his close he bumped into Mrs Finlay. He had his head down and she was under an umbrella. She was about to reprimand him for his clumsiness, for she was a nippy little woman, when she recognised him and was at once all solicitude. She put her gloved hand on his arm and stared at him with eyes "like a hungry cat's at a mouse" as Maggie had once described them. She was a widow who had once invited him to accompany her to Bingo. "What's wrong with that, Mr Hogg, if your wife won't go?" His friends in the *Airlie Arms* teased him about her. She lived up a tiled close in an adjacent street and could put on an accent to suit. Her husband had owned a plumber's business and left her money.

'I was terribly sorry to hear about poor Mrs Hogg,' she said. 'It must have been awful for you in that foreign place.'

He remembered it: the desert and the immense sky; the church with its Cross now straightened; the three old woman; the mongrel dog; the cludgy; old Joe and his bed; Elspeth so ill but undaunted; and Maggie dying so suddenly.

Yes, it had been awful, but it had been marvellous too; especially the blossoming of Maggie.

Mrs Finlay saw the tears in his eyes. She licked them up, as Maggie would have said, with her cat's tongue. 'Never mind. I know how you feel. It happened to me too. But life must go on. We'll have to see more of each other in the future.'

He nodded, not really agreeing to future assignations but merely agreeing that life must go on.

He got into the house safely, without being seen, as he thought; but within less than half an hour there was a timid knock on the door. It was wee Mrs Geddes, who lived on the same landing. She was white-haired and over seventy and she did everything timidly. Her man, Geordie, was bedridden. She had a son who she said was president of an oil company in Calgary, Canada. The very timidity of this boast made it almost convincing. Her clothes were always neat and clean but never new. Samuel, the tycoon, did not appear to be prodigal with what he sent her, if indeed he sent her anything. Geordie had worked for the bus company. They were an odd pair, but then, as Willie had once remarked to Maggie, up every close in Glasgow was to be found at least one odd pair.

'Pleased to see you back, Mr Hogg,' she whispered. 'Just to tell you there was a young man with red hair at your door. From the newspaper, he said. He said he would call back later.'

'Thanks, Mrs Geddes. How's Geordie?'

She put her face close to his. 'Still suffers terribly frae bed sores.'

Then she crept back to her own house, to put ointment on her man's painful backside.

Paint that, Mr Titian, Willie thought.

She was back in a minute, shocked by her own thoughtlessness. 'I forgot to say how sorry Geordie and me were to hear aboot poor Maggie. We're a' of us too taken up wi' oor ain misfortunes to remember ither folks'. But that'll no' happen to you, Mr Hogg. When you say you're sorry to hear aboot ither folks' trouble you mean it. It's a shame that this should hae happened to you.'

Then off she crept again.

He felt as if he had been blessed. He remembered Elspeth saying: 'You always tried to be a good man.'

His next visitor, alas, was Rab Butterworth, eighty years of age, with his teeth out as usual. They hurt him when they were in, so he kept them on the mantelpiece. He had once been a merchant seaman and had been to exotic places like Singapore and Hong Kong. His ship had never been blown up by a torpedo during the War but, as he often said, it could have been. He was very dark-skinned and was rumoured to have Lascar blood in him.

He was in a perpetual state of discontent. Luckily his wife Natalie was stone deaf. He had been talking to Meiklejohn.

'I telt him, Willie, that my life would mak' a mair interesting story than yours. I mean you were just a porter in a hospital. You never left Glasgow.'

'That's right, Rab. Whit did he say?'

'He didn't say a damned thing. He pretended no' to understaun' whit I was saying.'

Well, Rab, you do slobber and slaver. Maggie had never been able to make out a word you said.

Still, Willie had to live up to the reputation Mrs Geddes had given him. 'Why d'you want to get your name in the paper, Rab? It's no' important, is it?'

Rab was flabbergasted. He had always known that Willie Hogg was soft in the head but not quite as soft as this. Didn't he know that everybody wanted their name in the paper? That you were a nobody until you'd got your name in the paper, or better still had appeared on television? Was Willie going to appear on television?

'No' if I can help it, Rab.'

Rab went off champing his jaws. He had forgotten all about Maggie.

Mrs Jackson came next, with condolences and a bowl of greasy soup; this, by accident he supposed, was wrapped in a copy of the *Daily Chronicle* that contained the story of Maggie's death.

The article filled half a page. Willie was amazed to see a picture, blurred but recognisable, of the Mission at Red Bluffs. Meiklejohn must have got someone at Holbrook to take it and have it transmitted. He was certainly an enterprising young man. There were also pictures of Maggie and Willie. Maggie's death was described as a tragedy. So it had been but only to Willie. To the readers of the *Daily Chronicle*, as they read it at the breakfast table or in the lavatory or in the bus going to work it had merely been that day's sensation. The last paragraph gave the information that the funeral was to be in Janefield Cemetery on Wednesday at three o'clock. It was an invitation to the whole city to attend.

While reading all that, over and over again, he let the soup grow cold and therefore greasier, so that he had to pour it down the lavatory.

By eight o'clock he felt able to relax. No one would call now, not even a reporter. But at ten past there was a knock on the door, as peremptory as Mrs Geddes' had been timid.

It was a young man in a uniform.

'Mr William Hogg? ' he asked, briskly.

'That's me.'

'Sign here, please.'

Willie signed and then was handed a cablegram. He already knew what it had to tell him.

And so it turned out. 'REGRET ELSPETH DIED RANDY'. That was all.

Willie sat down. His legs had gone weak. He crushed the cablegram. He needed company. He would have been glad to see a bluebottle. Maggie had never been able to sleep if there was a bluebottle buzzing in the bedroom.

Both sisters were gone. He would miss Elspeth as much as he was missing Maggie. During those few days at the Mission he had got to know and admire her.

He smoothed out the cablegram and then placed it on the mantel-piece, beside the photograph of him and Maggie in Rothesay.

'Weel Maggie,' he said, 'that's Elspeth gone. She wasn't long after you.'

But was Elspeth now in heaven, welcomed by bands of angels, while poor Maggie, thanks to him, was kept outside the gates?

What nonsense, he thought, but not as scornfully as before.

He could not bear to stay in the house. He would go out, jump on a bus, get off in some part of the city where he wasn't known, go into a pub there, sit in a corner, listen to the chatter about him, and sip his beer. He wouldn't be noticed. Lonely old men were to be found in every pub in the city. Nobody bothered them. Whatever their griefs they were given peace to endure them.

5

Meiklejohn came next morning at half-past nine, looking prosperous in a fur hat and sheepskin coat, but also bleary-eyed. He hadn't had much sleep, he explained. He had just come from reporting a murder in Ayrshire. A farm labourer had cut his wife's throat with a blunt heuk, out of jealousy. She had been having an affair with a farmer who kept pigs. Meiklejohn had brought with him a copy of the morning's paper. His story about the murder was on the front page. There was also a photograph of the murdered woman, with her neck intact, and of her murderer when he had been her happy and loving bride-groom.

Willie felt infinitely sad. He chided Meiklejohn for his apparent callousness.

'Hell, Willie, these things are our bread and butter, didn't you know? They're what people like to read about. They sell newspapers.'

'God help us all then.'

'So you've become religious, Willie?'

'It depends on whit you mean by religious.'

'We'll not go into that, Willie. Now, about the funeral tomorrow. You're not really expecting it to be private, in the ordinary sense of the word?'

'Why no'?'

'Because, Willie, it belongs to Glasgow, Maggie's funeral. Yesterday I spoke to some of your neighbours. They all said they would like to attend, to show their respect and liking for you. So we're proposing eight cars, at our expense, the best the undertaker can lay his hands on. He tells me, by the way, that flowers are flooding in.'

'I said no flowers.'

'See what I mean, Willie? Fewer than eight would be underdoing it, more would be overdoing it. Eight's just right, wouldn't you say?'

'There's going to be only one car, Mr Meiklejohn.'

'And who's going to be in it with you? That old boozer I met in the pub? What was his name? Charlie McCann.'

'Charlie and two ithers. My freends. I haven't asked them yet but if they're no' willing I'll go on my ain.'

'Don't do that, Willie. You're not thinking clearly. Grief's clouding your judgment.'

'I've had enough publicity, Mr Meiklejohn.'

'That's just it, Willie. If you turn up by yourself or with three old boozers publicity is just what you'll get, lots of it.'

'Why do you ca' them old boozers? They're honourable men.'

'Another thing, Willie. Mr Chalmers, the undertaker, tells me there's to be no minister present.'

'Whit aboot it?'

'Now if you know a better way of attracting publicity I'd like you to tell me. Funerals with ministers take place every day of the week, dozens of them, up and down the country, and nobody pays them the slightest bit of attention; but there's none at all or damned few with no minister. I know you're not a member of a church and so haven't got a minister of your own but there are free lances. You'll have heard of the Rev. Angus Turnbull?'

Willie scowled. He had not only heard of Turnbull, he had heard him. He had been M.C. at a charity concert. During the course of his remarks, which were frequent for he loved the sound of his own voice, he had cracked jokes which had seemed to Willie indecent. Willie had been outraged. He had appealed to Maggie beside him but she had seldom seen the point of any joke, whatever its colour. Other women near him, however, older than himself, white-haired and prim-looking, had squealed with laughter, when they ought to have been silently wrathful. They had kept referring to the clown in the white collar as "Awful Angus".

Willie would sooner have had the Pope or the Grandmaster of the Orange Lodge at Maggie's grave than the Rev. Angus Turnbull.

'He's got a great sense of humour for a minister, Willie. Not only that he's got what's called the common touch. He can have people laughing one minute and in tears the next. They say that when he speaks at a graveside even the worms are impressed.'

Willie felt sorry for any worms that had to listen to Mr Turnbull. He said so.

'I didn't think you were as bigotted as that, Willie.'

The word jarred. Was it justified? Were what he called his principles not principles at all but prejudices? Was he being not resolute as he liked to think but pig-headed?

'If there's to be no minister, Willie, who's going to speak? Surely there must be some words spoken? Maggie deserves that.'

'I'll speak them myself.'

'You, Willie?'

'Wha kent her best? Wha loved her maist? Wha was wi' her when she dee'd?' He was almost in tears. 'That was whit she wanted.'

'I appreciate that, Willie, but what if you broke down and couldn't speak? It wouldn't be the first time that a husband went to pieces at his wife's graveside.'

'Whit would be wrang wi' that? Whit if I did break doon and weep? People would understand.'

'They'd understand all right and they'd enjoy it; some of them anyway. Ghouls.'

Willie was astonished at the reporter's vehemence.

'In my job, Willie, you learn what people are like.'

'I'm a lot aulder than you, Mr Meiklejohn. I think I ken whit people are like; mair likely to dae a good turn than a bad.'

'A lot of them will think they have a right to be present at the funeral, Willie.'

'You mean those who sent me money?'

'Yes, Willie. They'll think they've paid the admission fee.'

It could be true in some cases but Willie was sad to hear a young man being so cynical.

'If the *Chronicle* wanted an exclusive, Willie, would you let us have it? For a price of course.'

'Whit's an exclusive?'

'Exclusive right to publish your story. You know, your private thoughts, your plans for the future, what happened at the Mission. If we thought it good copy we'd pay well.'

'I don't want any more money or any more publicity. After the funeral naebody will ever hear of Willie Hogg.'

'I hope you're not intending to do something drastic, Willie.'

'Like jumping aff Dalmarnock Bridge? Wouldn't that be a great exclusive? No, Mr Meiklejohn, I just meant I'll become one of the crowd, of nae interest to newspapers. Don't be disappointed, there's sure to be another murder or rape or bank robbery round the corner.'

As soon as he said it he was ashamed. He had rebuked this young man for being cynical and here he was being cynical himself.

'I'm just doing my job, Willie. Think it over. I'll drop in tomorrow morning to see if you've changed your mind. The Rev. Angus is always available.'

'You ken, Mr Meiklejohn, you haven't asked aboot Elspeth.'

'Elspeth? Who's she? Oh yes, Maggie's sister, the one that has cancer. How is she?'

'She's deid. I got a cable yesterday. Would you like to see it?'

He took it from the mantelpiece and handed it to the reporter.

For almost a minute Meiklejohn said nothing. The cynicism and self-interest drained out of his face. 'I'm sorry, Willie.' He picked up his hat from the table. 'I'm truly sorry.'

Then he was gone.

6

After one of the longest and most difficult days of his life Willie set out in the evening for the *Airlie Arms*, wearing his week-day clothes. It wasn't raining but the pavements still glistened. The shop windows were lit, always a reassuring sight. He felt light-headed and a bit agitated. The events of the past few days had been too much for him. If his friends rejected him, if they had not got over their huff, he might break down, but if he did it would be inwardly. Outwardly he would put on a display of gallusness. Hadn't Elspeth called him a gallus wee Glasgow keelie? He would order them whiskies, malts at that, and if they were refused he would drink them himself. But surely Maggie's death would have made a difference, though to be truthful they hadn't known her all that well, just as he didn't know Alec's wife or Angus's all that well or Charlie's cat.

He turned the corner at Wallace Street and got a shock. In that area of buildings condemned or already demolished the pub had been an oasis of light and life, but this evening it was dark and deserted. It wasn't shut because of a holiday, surely. Had the hours of opening been changed again? He wouldn't have been surprised. The self-important guardians in their golden chambers were too fond of issuing such orders.

A man was approaching. He looked as if he would know about the destiny of pubs. He did too, and explained, with fervent obscenities. 'Aye, mister, the whale fucking building's to be knocked doon next week, by order of the fucking cooncil. It's a fucking shame. There's been a pub here since I was born. That's fucking progress for you.'

Willie thanked him and then felt as desolate in that dark city street as he had done in the shining desert, after Maggie's death. Here was the traveller returned to his well-loved oasis, to find the well dry, the palm trees withered, the tents struck, and his comrades gone. Where could he himself go now? A daft thought came to him and was at once dismissed as daft thoughts should be. Why not go to Mrs Finlay's tiled close and knock on her door that was sure to have her name in fancy letters on a brass plate? A much more sensible idea followed and this he acted upon. He would look in some other pubs in the neighbourhood, in the hope that his friends might have found a new howff in one of them. The *Auld Hoose* was the most likely. It had secluded corners and was comfortably old-fashioned, with no juke-box.

It might though be a perilous quest, for he would be known in most of the pubs and would be offered drinks. It would be churlish to decline those liquid condolences, so that he might have to be sent home in a taxi. What a disgrace, to be drunk on the evening before his wife's funeral. He remembered that Mrs Finlay did not approve of strong drink. 'Just a wee sherry at the New Year, Mr Hogg.'

He was in luck or rather his instincts did not let him down. There, in the *Auld Hoose*, in a snug alcove, sat his cronies, so like themselves that he couldn't help smiling; so much so that they stared back at him with frowns of puzzlement and disapproval, why was a man so recently bereaved showing such levity?

He smiled at the barman, Jimmy McFarlane, who smiled back. 'They've been expecting you, Willie,' he said.

Angus made room for him. He sat down.

He looked at them and they looked at him. He was now close to tears and so were they. Angus patted Willie's hand.

Charlie signalled to the barman.

'No, the drinks are on me tonight,' said Willie.

'Go and get the man his pint, Alec,' said Charlie.

'With pleasure,' said Alec.

Other customers were looking across. 'Sorry aboot your wife, Willie,' said one. The rest nodded agreement.

Willie felt embarrassed but at the same time consoled. He was a Glasgow man and here were Glasgow men honouring him and Maggie.

He remembered the Indians dancing in front of the church.

'I went alang to the *Arms*,' he said. 'It was shut.'

'They're starting on the demolition next week,' said Alec.

'But you're cosy enough here.'

'We've been made very welcome,' said Angus.

'Thanks to you, Willie,' said Charlie.

'Me? Whit had I to dae wi' it?'

'I'm no' saying you're famous. I take that back, Willie. It was a bloody mean thing to say. But you've been in everybody's thochts.'

'It must have been hard for you oot there,' said Alec.

Willie nodded. It had been very hard. He remembered Maggie putting her arms round his neck and whispering: 'Oh Willie,' and Elspeth, dying but finding the courage to take back a lie and tell the truth.

'The funeral's the morrow,' he said.

'It was in the paper,' said Alec.

'You want it to be private, Willie?' said Angus.

'Aye. Just my freends. You three, and Duncan, but I don't suppose he's been aroon'.'

'Disappeared completely,' said Charlie.

'We've been wondering, Willie, who'd be at it,' said Alec. 'You've got nae relations so far as we ken and we couldnae think of ony that Maggie had, save her sister and she's faur away.'

'Elspeth's deid,' said Willie. He had brought the cablegram. He showed it to them.

They stared at it.

'This Randy, is he her man?' asked Angus.

'Aye. Randolph Hansen.'

'Hansen?' said Alec. 'That's a Norwegian name.'

'She'll be buried in America?' said Charlie.

'Aye. So I'm relying on you three.'

'I never gang to funerals,' said Charlie. 'You ken that, Willie.'

'I ken that, Charlie, but I hope you'll gang to this one.'

'I've got nae black suit fit for a funeral.'

'A' you need nooadays is a black tie,' said Alec.

'I havenae got a black tie.'

'I'll lend you one. I've got twa.'

'Will you come then, Charlie? I want you to. I need you to. Please. The morrow at three. A car will pick you up.'

'There's just one thing, Willie,' said Angus. 'I ken your views aboot religion and I respect them, but you've got to respect mine too.'

'I always have, Angus.'

'That's true. Will there be a minister at the graveside, saying a few words? He doesnae have to be a Catholic priest.'

'No, Angus, there will be nae minister.'

The other two, Charlie and Alec, looked uncomfortable but not shocked and miserable like Angus. They would have had a minister if they had been in Willie's place, but it would have been for appearance's sake, since they didn't believe in God or heaven any more than he did. They were worried that Willie, though they admired him for sticking to his principles, might rue it afterwards. They knew what a tender conscience he had.

'Is it whit Maggie would have wanted?' asked Charlie.

'It is.'

'Are you sure?' asked Alec.

'I'm sure.'

'I'd like to come,' said Angus, 'but I don't see how I can.'

'Whit's preventing you?' asked Charlie, dourly.

'Weel, you see, Charlie, I was brought up a believer and I still am a believer, maist o' the time onyway.'

'Whit has that got to dae wi' it?' asked Charlie.

'Wouldn't I be taking part in a denial of God?'

'But there's naething to stop you,' said Willie, 'from making your ain private arrangements wi' God. You could pray to him, couldn't you, in to yourself?'

Angus was satisfied. 'You're a good man, Willie. You say you don't believe in God but I tell you this, God believes in you.'

Willie felt foolish but pleased.

'Is there naebody going to speak?' asked Alec.

'I am.'

'You, Willie?'

They all looked anxious. Willie was a sly wee bugger at times. He used big words they'd never heard of. In an argument he would mention the names of philosphers. He often visited the Art Galleries. He'd been twice to the Burrell Collection. He had books at home, and a dictionary. He watched programmes on television about science and nature. But despite all that what was he really? Their crony, who like them had left school at fourteen and had won no prizes there. He was just not qualified to make an address at a funeral, even if the dead person was his wife, and especially if, as they feared, a big crowd turned up.

'Dae you ken whit you're going to say?' asked Charlie.

'Hae you been rehearsing?' asked Alec.

'I'm going to read a poem,' said Willie.

'A poem!' Charlie was astounded. Poems, except for some by Robert Burns, were not for the ordinary working man. You had to have been at University to be able to understand poems.

'Whit poem?' asked Alec. He wasn't quite as sceptical as Charlie. He still remembered poems he had learned at school. No wonder, for they had been leathered into him. There was one about a woman being drowned in the Highlands and there was young Lochinvar who had rescued his sweetheart just as she was being married to a man she didn't love. They were good poems but not suitable to be read at a funeral.

'It's ca'd "What has she lost?" That's the first line.'

'Did you see it in a magazine?' asked Charlie.

'I heard the man who wrote it reciting it, in a pub aboot two years ago. He handed out copies.'

'A pub?' said Alec. 'Whit pub?'

'In Paisley.'

'Paisley? Dae you mean to say you went a' the way to Paisley to listen to poems in a pub?' Charlie was incredulous and stern.

Willie was a little shame-faced. He never liked to appear intellectually pretentious. 'It's a pub famous for inviting poets to read their poems.'

'You never asked us to go wi' you,' said Alec. 'No' that we would hae gone, mind you.'

Angus sneered. 'Whit kind of fellow was he, this poet? Wi' hair doon to his shoulders?'

'No, Angus.' But didn't Jesus Christ have hair down to his shoulders? 'His hair was as short as your ain, but whiter.'

'So he was auld?'

'Aye, Charlie. His ain wife had just dee'd, like Maggie of a heart attack. Whit his poem's aboot is whit a deid person has lost. Wi' respect to you, Angus, I don't believe myself that daith gies us onything, it just takes everything away. That's why life is tragic.'

Not even Angus was going to deny that.

'Whit do you say,' said Charlie, 'if we hae anither half-pint? My mooth's gone dry.'

It was agreed. It was also agreed that Willie should pay for the extra drinks. After all it was he who'd made their mouths dry.

When they had their fresh half-pints in front of them Alec said:
'Could you gie us a wee taste o' this poem, Willie? So we can tell you
if we think it's suitable.'

'Go on, Willie,' said the others.

Willie stared at his beer but saw Maggie's face.

> 'What has she lost?
> All the people she loved.
> All the people who loved her.
> All the strangers laughing
> In the streets and shops.

That's how it starts.'

'Aye,' said Charlie.

'Weel,' said Alec.

Angus just sighed.

All three of them were thinking that not many people had loved
poor Maggie, nor had she loved many herself, and as for strangers no
woman had avoided them more. Now if the poem had been about
Willie himself it would have been more truthful.

They couldn't very well say that to him. He was too close to tears.
In fact he got up to go to the toilet where he would dry his eyes.

'Weel, Charlie, whit do you think?' asked Alec. 'Should we tell him
he'd be wiser to read a bit oot o' the Bible?'

'No. Let him read his poem. Naebody will understand it onyway.'

'And no' many will hear it,' said Angus. 'It being in the open air, wi'
the wind blawing maybe, and Willie's no' got a loud voice.'

Willie came back, smiling bravely.

They asked him about the Mission. They were particularly interested in old Joe or Thundercloud and his bed, but most of all in Willie's
reason for wanting to straighten the Cross before he left.

He didn't know himself.

'Maybe it's because I've always had a tidy nature.'

'Was it no' to show respect for your sister-in-law?'

'It could hae been that, Alec.'

'I think it was to show respect for God. Say whit you like, Willie,
everybody's born wi' a respect for God.'

'You could be right, Angus.'

7

Wednesday, the day of the funeral, was dull but dry in the morning. The weather forecast on the radio was hopeful: there might be showers in the afternoon but they would be light and there was a possibility of some sunshine. Willie wondered if undertakers like farmers and fishermen got special reports, but wouldn't they have to go out and do their work whatever the conditions? What though if the grave was water-logged or the ground too hard to dig? Geordie Geddes had once told him that in places in mid-Canada bodies had to be kept in refrigerators for months until the thaw came.

His mind kept bringing up irrelevant things like that.

There was no visit from Meiklejohn. Either he had decided to leave Willie in peace or, more likely, had come to realise that Willie was simply one of millions whose hour of importance, if it could be called that, would soon be over and then he would be one of Glasgow's lonely old men, of no interest even to himself.

Willie felt he had to go along to the undertaker's to make sure that his wishes and not the newspaper's were to be carried out: one car and not eight. It was chilly, so he was able to hide most of his face behind a big woollen muffler. Nobody gave him a second glance.

He was lucky to catch Mr Chalmers in the shop. He was about to go out to arrange another funeral. Somehow this busyness of undertakers was a comfort to Willie, not because he meanly felt his own bereavement was easier to bear if others were suffering too, but because it made him feel part of humanity, sharer of its tribulations.

Dressed in striped trousers and black jacket – what a contrast to Mr Bellingham! – and with his hair so glossy flies could have skated on it, Mr Chalmers asked Willie into his office. He himself sat down and took from a drawer a packet of cigarettes. He lit one and puffed desperately, as if he was saving his life instead of shortening it. Willie marvelled that a man who had buried so many victims of smoking should smoke himself.

'I've come, Mr Chalmers, to make sure of the arrangements. There's just to be the one car.'

'Not eight?' Mr Chalmers smiled. He was happier now, with his lungs a little bit blacker.

'Just the one. For me and three of my freends. Here are their addresses.' He put a sheet of paper on the desk. 'I'd like them to be picked up.'

'It shall be done.'

'Aboot flowers. I was told lots have been sent.'

'That is so.'

'Weel, I'd like them sent to city hospitals, wi' cards saying "In memory of Margaret Hogg" '

'Margaret?'

'Aye. Put the expense on my bill.'

The Fund would pay. After all the journey wasn't over until Maggie was buried.

'No flowers at all, Mr Hogg?'

'Just the bunch of red roses I sent yesterday. Did they come?'

'They did. Is there anything else?'

'You're remembering there's to be nae minister?'

'Yes, I remember.'

'I'm going to say a few words myself. I'll read a poem.'

'Written by yourself, Mr Hogg?'

'No, no. A real poem.'

Mr Chalmers had already puffed through one cigarette and was on to his second. 'Have you considered, Mr Hogg, that it will be an ordeal for you? You are not, if I may say so, a young man.'

'I ken that.'

But nobody, and certainly not an undertaker smoking himself to death, could help or reassure him. Even if all of Glasgow was present he would be on his own.

'That's a' then,' he said, rising.

At the door he turned. 'Would you please tell the driver to tak us afterwards to the *Auld Hoose*?'

'That's the public house in Scott Street? He will be so instructed.'

'Thanks.'

'Good luck, Mr Hogg.'

But what, in the circumstances, would constitute good luck? That he didn't wet himself from nervousness? Didn't go to pieces and weep like a wean? Didn't fall into the grave? Didn't drop the paper with the poem written on it?

He might have added, wasn't invited to lunch by Mrs McBride. Her house was a scandal for untidiness and smell. She wore the same apron for weeks and wiped her nose on it. Mice were said to dine on the fat in her frying-pan.

She knocked on his door just after twelve.

'Sam and me wad like you to come and hae a bite wi' us, Willie. Naething fancy, you ken. Just tatties and mince and a glass o' beer.'

He managed to get out of it without hurting her feelings, though most of her neighbours would have said she had no feelings to hurt. Insults stotted off her. He murmured sadly he had no appetite and needed to be alone. He was sure she would understand.

She said she did. He wasn't sure whether she was going to blow her nose or kiss him. She blew her nose and then she kissed him.

When she was gone he sat and looked up at Maggie's photograph on the mantelpiece.

If you'd accepted, Willie, I've never have spoken to you again.

But she offered oot o' kindness.

When did I ever say that sluts couldn't be kind?

I never heard you say it, Maggie.

But she's got nae right to ask folk to eat in her hoose till she's scrubbed it frae top to bottom.

That's so.

Maggie looked satisfied but not smug. She had never looked smug in her life.

8

Promptly at half-past two the big black Rolls Royce stopped outside the close and with a toot suited to its opulence let Willie know it was there.

Before leaving the house he held Maggie's photograph in his hands and gazed at it. This was to give him courage. Yet what good was courage? All it did was help him to bear the pain of his loss; it could not lessen it. Nothing, not even time, could do that. Time indeed would only increase it, for every day would bring fresh reminders of the void.

Still, there was dignity in courage, so he went down the stairs with his head high.

There were only two women at the closemouth. They were Mrs Morrison and Mrs King, incorrigible nosey-parkers. Other neighbours were keeping out of the way, with their curtains drawn. This pair didn't throw confetti at him but they looked as if they would have liked to. There had been a wedding a week ago, with a car like that at the close-mouth, and they had thrown handfuls. 'All the best, Mr Hogg,' said Mrs Morrison, and Mrs King, a little more appropriately, said, 'You're getting a guid day for it onyway,' for it so happened that the sun had begun to shine.

The chauffeur was Mr Jeffrey who had driven the black van from Prestwick. He was wearing his uniform now and Willie saw the reason for the long sideburns: they went well with the black hat and jacket. He held the door open for Willie and gave him a little bow, as if this were 10 Downing Street and Willie was Prime Minister. He smiled too, but it was a smile more in keeping with the occasion than another man's greeting face would have been. It was the fruit of much practice at many funerals, that smile.

Willie himself was wearing a dark-grey suit that he had bought more than thirty years ago. Maggie had helped him choose it. It was now unfashionable, with turn-ups and buttoned flies; it also smelled of moth-balls. His shirt was white and his tie black. He had spent an hour in pressing suit and shirt. He carried his raincoat over his arm; his cap was in the pocket. After it was over he would walk home from the *Auld Hoose*. It might be raining by then.

Alec and Angus were waiting at the former's close-mouth. They were more suitably dressed for a funeral than Willie himself, but then they had had their wives to supervise them. Their suits did not smell of moth-balls and were more neatly pressed. Alec's was dark-blue and Angus's black. In his button-hole Angus had a small silver crucifix.

'I hope you don't mind, Willie,' he said.

'Why should I mind, Angus?'

'Thanks, Willie.'

The next stop was outside Charlie's close-mouth, in a not so respectable street. Obscene graffiti covered the walls.

To their relief Charlie was waiting for them.

Relief quickly turned to dismay.

'My God,' muttered Alec, not at all blasphemously. He really was invoking divine help.

Charlie was wearing a navy-blue blazer with gilt buttons, one of which was missing. He had bought it at a jumble sale years ago. Since he had shrunk somewhat in the meantime it hung loosely on him, as did, even more so, his off-white flannel trousers; these had a conspicuous stain on the left knee. An attempt had been made to iron them, by Charlie himself, so that instead of one crease each leg had several. Blazer and trousers were covered with cat hairs. He wore no socks and his shoes were bauchles, chosen not for appearance but for comfort, since they were wide enough for him to slip on without having to bend, and they accommodated his bunions. His shirt was pink. His scalp gleamed. The age marks were prominent.

He noticed the horrified scrutinies. 'Will I dae?' he asked, humorously, as he climbed in.

'You'll dae fine, Charlie,' said Willie.

They were now making for the undertaker's.

Charlie grinned. 'Is that a medal you're wearing, Angus?'

'You can see it's no' a medal,' said Angus.

'Whaur are *your* medals, Alec?'

Alec was proud of his war medals.

He refused to answer this mischievous question.

'You wore them on Armistice Day.'

'That was different.'

'I thocht *that* was a kind o' funeral, remembering millions.'

Alec and Angus exchanged worried glances. Charlie was in one of his awkward moods. Willie didn't seem to mind, but perhaps he was too perturbed to notice.

They arrived at the undertaker's. The hearse was waiting. On top of the coffin or casket was the bunch of red roses.

There were dozens, no hundreds, of people, men and women, mostly elderly.

'I thocht it was to be private,' said Charlie. He waved to the crowd.

'Is it somebody you ken?' asked Alec. He thought this waving was vulgar.

'The Queen doesnae ken everybody she waves to, does she?'

Alec looked hard at Willie. Charlie would have to be restrained. There wasn't a smell of drink off him; there was a smell of cat but not of drink. He was being deliberately troublesome. He might turn the whole thing into a pantomime if he wasn't stopped in time and Willie showed no sign of wanting to stop him.

Willie had a strange look in his eyes as he gazed out at the people lining the streets all the way to the cemetery.

Many of the women had handkerchiefs at their eyes.

'It was damned embarrassing, Sadie,' Alec was to say to his wife later. 'You'd have thought we were royalty.'

'You were better than royalty,' she was to retort, making him wonder what the hell she meant.

Charlie kept waving, with variations. This, he would say, is how the Duke does it. This is Charles's style.

Alec could stand it no longer. 'You shouldnae be waving at a', Charlie.'

'Why no'?'

'This isnae a celebration.' Surely, he would have liked to say, you remember your own wife's funeral, even if it was fifty years ago. 'Think of Willie's feelings.'

'Wave if you like, Charlie,' said Willie.

He was remembering that Maggie had called Charlie a smelly old baboon. She had been sorry afterwards but amends had never been made.

'I wouldnae like to hurt your feelings, Willie.'

Willie loved his friend then. He knew now what Charlie had been suffering all those years.

The crowd was thick at the cemetery gates.

'Christ, Angus,' muttered Alec, 'if I'd kent there was going to be a multitude I don't think I'd have come.'

If Maggie had known, thought Willie, she wouldn't have come either. He smiled at his own silly joke.

His friends were alarmed. They thought he was going to break down.

There were crowds in the cemetery itself, among the tombstones. Those with places nearest to the grave must have come early.

One of them, at the very front, was Mrs Finlay, wearing a red raincoat with hat to match.

He knew then that nobody would ever take Maggie's place.

'Are you a' right, Willie?' asked Angus. He would dearly have liked to slip his crucifix into Willie's hand.

The four old men got out, stiffly. The chauffeur assisted them. The sun was shining.

Alec noticed some people among the watchers grin when they saw Charlie. Surely it was a mistake to have invited him, he was to tell Sadie later. No, it wasn't, she was to reply. You didn't desert your friends because they were old and stupid.

Willie saw Meiklejohn among the crowd. He had his fur hat in his hand. It looked as if he was there as a friend, not as a reporter.

Meanwhile the coffin was being lifted out of the hearse. The roses stayed put.

Smelling of hair-oil and cigarettes, Mr Chalmers stood behind Willie. 'Everything is ready, Mr Hogg,' he whispered.

Willie glanced down and saw a worm. He looked round and saw some finches waiting in a bush.

The coffin was lowered into the grave. Willie and his three friends, Mr Chalmers himself, and the chauffeur, all bare-headed, held the cords. The grave-diggers stood by lest a snag occurred. None did.

In the silence a woman sobbed and a child cried. The noise of traffic could be heard; the city elsewhere was getting on with its life.

It was time for Willie to speak. He was hesitant at first.

'I would like to thank you a' for coming here on this cauld day to help me bury my wife Maggie. You werenae invited but that doesnae mean you're no' welcome. Glesca folk ken when to come and when to stay away. This was a time to come.'

He paused. They're wondering why there's no minister, he thought. They're thinking I must be a thrawn, bigotted old bugger. They could be right.

'As you maybe ken Maggie died in Arizona, thoosands o' miles away. She wanted to be buried here beside her faither and mither, so I brought her hame. She was a woman who found life difficult at times, but at the end she seemed to find herself and was happy. It was a sad time at the Mission where we were visiting her sister Elspeth, a Glasgow woman herself. She's deid too. She dee'd twa days after Maggie. Maggie was the best of us at the end. The Indians stood ootside the church where she was lying and chanted a song of grief. I'm told it was a great honour. I was very proud of her.'

He paused again. Many of them thought he would not be able to go on.

His voice was loud and clear.

'I would like to read a poem. The man who wrote it had just lost his wife, like me. It says whit I feel and says it better than I ever could.

> ' "What has she lost?
> All the people she loved
> All the people who loved her.
> All the strangers
> Laughing in the streets and shops.
> All the birds of the garden,
> The acrobatic tits
> The jealous robins
> And the chirpy finches,
> But also
> The eagles in their eyries
> The capercaillies in the wood
> And the swans on the river.
> All the animals, the cattle
> And their calves, the sheep
> And their lambs, the deer
> That leapt the fence
> And the rabbits
> That ate the nasturtiums,
> But also
> The tigers in their jungles
> And the elephants
> On their African plains.
> All the fishes of the sea.
> All the pests, the bluebottle
> That buzzed in the bedroom
> The midges that tormented
> The fleas in Lucy's fur
> And the ticks on the deer.
> The whole living world
> Is what she has lost
> And I have lost it too
> For it was contained in her." '

When he finished there was silence. Were they still waiting for a mention of God? But surely if they were true believers they must have found Him in the poem?

He looked up at them. He wished them all well, but he saw what the poet had meant. Without Maggie to love and cherish, to go home to, and to discuss things with, joy had gone out of his life. A part of him had died with her.

He threw his handful of earth and turned away towards the car. Remembering that he was still, as it were, the host, he stood aside and let his friends climb in first. This time they were glad of the chauffeur's assistance.

In a minute they were on their way, carefully because of the people thronging the avenue.

Tears were running down Angus's fat cheeks. 'When did Maggie ever see a capercaillie?' he asked.

'She could have,' said Charlie.

Yes, that was it, she could have when she was alive but she never could now.

Willie himself could, but where would be the pleasure if he could not share it with her?

Charlie patted him on the knee. 'You'll get ower it, Willie.'

But Charlie, after fifty years, have you got over it?

'You did very well, Willie,' said Alec.

They were now out of the cemetery and heading, no longer at a funereal pace, towards the *Auld Hoose*.